the burden of light

MICHAEL BUHLER

◆ FriesenPress

One Printers Way
Altona, MB R0G0B0,
Canada

www.friesenpress.com

Photo credit for the cover belongs to Brian Jones.

Drink the Hemlock Books
www.drinkthehemlockbooks.com

ISBN
978-1-03-910928-5 (Hardcover)
978-1-03-910927-8 (Paperback)
978-1-03-910929-2 (eBook)

Fiction, Short Stories (Single Author)

Distributed to the trade by The Ingram Book Company

Table of Contents

Introduction

An old legend has it that as a young man, Saint Christopher wanted to serve the strongest ruler on earth. He wandered across the known world until he came to a vast kingdom led by a wealthy and powerful king. Christopher asked the people if this was the strongest ruler on earth, and they all said yes, he was. Christopher was a six-foot-eight, three-hundred-pound Persian, with muscles like an ox. When he told the king that he wanted to serve him, the king was elated. Immediately, Christopher was placed in the king's bodyguard.

For years he served faithfully, until one day he saw his king tremble with fear when told the devil was roving through his kingdom. This caused confusion for Christopher. How could the strongest ruler on earth be scared of the devil? Obviously, the devil must be more powerful than the king he served. So, Christopher abandoned his king and went in search of Satan.

For years he wandered through cities and wilderness, until one day he met a band of ruffians. They were fierce, and wandered the earth unopposed by any king or army, but when their leader saw the mighty Persian before them, he couldn't help but be curious.

"What are you doing in this wilderness?" asked the leader.

"I wish to serve the devil, so I am searching for him," said Christopher.

"Well! You have found him! I am the devil," the leader exclaimed jubilantly. So, Christopher wandered the earth with the ruffian gang, causing chaos wherever they went.

While walking down the road one day, Christopher saw the devil move in fear to avoid passing a roadside shrine. This caused Christopher to wonder once again. Why had the devil shown fear? He approached the shrine, and saw that it was placed in honour of the Christ.

"Why did you avoid that shrine dedicated to the Christ?" Christopher asked the devil.

"Christ—keep him far away," muttered the devil, with a deep frustration that caused the road to shake.

Once more Christopher's logic suggested to him that the Christ must be more powerful than Satan if a mere roadside shrine could cause the devil to tremble. So it was that Christopher left the devil, in search of the Christ.

After many years of searching, one day Christopher approached a river, beside which was a small hut where a hermit lived.

Christopher peered carefully into the hut.

"Who are you looking for?" asked the hermit.

"I am searching for the Christ," he said. "I wish to serve him."

"I serve the Christ," said the hermit.

"Can I stay with you, then, so I also can learn how to serve the Christ?" asked Christopher.

"By all means. I fast six days a week, read the Holy Gospels, and pray. On Sunday, I break my fast in celebration of God's gifts by eating bread and wild grapes."

"I am a six-foot-eight, three-hundred-pound man with muscles like an ox," replied Christopher, with some fear. "I don't know if I can fast for six days a week."

"Well," said the hermit, "to serve the Christ, why don't you help people cross the river? Many people lose their possessions while crossing the river. Some people even drown. That would be a wonderful way to serve the Christ."

Christopher agreed, and over the next number of years he helped people at the crossing. One day as he sat praying by the river, a child approached him.

"I wish to cross the river," the child said.

Christopher stood up and put the small child on his shoulders. They entered the river and began to cross. As Christopher neared the middle of the river, the current began to grow stronger, and the water began to rise higher, passing his chin and reaching his nose. While Christopher laboured against the current and the rising waters, he began to sink beneath the weight of the child, who was growing heavier and heavier. Christopher fought with all his might, digging his staff into the riverbed and propelling himself forward in a desperate attempt to save the child's life. Eventually, Christopher won the struggle with the river, and with the weight of the child lightening, he clambered up the far river bank, exhausted.

"I felt like I had the weight of the universe on my back," he exclaimed with awe.

"You did," said the child. "I am the creator of heaven and earth—I am the Christ, whom you serve."

Christopher served the Christ with renewed vigour for many more years, to the day of his death, when he was martyred.

This old tale suggests we are called to be "Christ-bearers." We are called to not only look in thanksgiving for the good around us and within us, but to carry the good on this earth, and to participate in co-creating the good, incarnating it. We are called to be bearers of divine light. The freedom and responsibility that human beings have been given alongside this calling can be a great burden. After all, this calling is only an invitation, not an order, and there is no promise of reward in this lifetime. In fact, there may not be any reward for being a Christ-bearer. It is a labour of love.

In his novel *The Brothers Karamazov,* Dostoyevsky's Grand Inquisitor charged the Christ with offering too much freedom to human beings. In fact, the Grand Inquisitor thought this freedom had messed us up, because it is so easy to reject the call and the responsibility to carry the divine light. The moment we turn from the invitation, we are left in darkness. The solution the Inquisitor had for our restoration was to take away some of our freedom. Keep us well fed, and keep us within a collective group with rigid laws, and we will be happier and better behaved.

Most certainly, human freedom, which includes being a self-conscious person with a free will and a conscience, is a difficult "gift" to handle. The characters in this collection of short stories are broken people living broken lives. Some are closer, or more open, to God's grace than others, and some are openly resistant to the call to be a Christ-bearer. Is there a character or event to be found in each story through whom grace seeks to touch a human soul?

I appreciate the time you spend reading. Thank you for the time you give to these stories. An old Jewish proverb says there are twelve Holy People in each generation carrying our human community, like pillars holding up a bridge. I cannot help but wonder if those who carefully read books play a similar role in enriching our communities.

I would like to thank my wife Rena, and my children Aidan and Jack, for their love and support. I would like to thank author Paul Toffanello for his many hours of editorial support over the years. I would also like to thank Laura Kelly for her love of reading and writing, and for being a sympathetic reader and editor over the years. Other people whose editorial contributions have helped me along the way are Rena, my daughter Aidan, and my friend Don Lee. I am richly blessed.

All good wishes,
MJB, December 2020

The Red Canoe

Parts One and Two

Part 1: Withdrawal

The narrow river was deep, and the current was weak. The hot sun made everything bright, but the water appeared almost black. Thomas didn't have any interest in the bright shore, or the trees that reflected the light. But he did feel like jumping into the darkness that was the river.

In front of him was Moses, paddling half-heartedly. Moses was a very noble name, but the man before him had failed to live up to it, so everyone called him Moss. They were quiet for the most part. Sometimes a raven cawed, and a short time earlier they had startled a mother duck with her ducklings. Later, though, a bull moose would come crashing through the bush and into the dark river. It swam with purpose across the river, with the sound of a steam boat. Thomas urged the canoe forward to get closer, but Moss was frightened by the size of the bull, and stuck his paddle into the water to break their quickening drift.

They came to a thick log jam, and were forced to unload the canoe before dragging it over. But when they reached the top of the log jam, they saw so much debris upriver that they were forced to portage through cedar swamp. Thomas cut a trail with a machete, and Moss came behind, making marks on tree trunks with an axe so they would find their way back for the canoe. The sun was hot, and the mosquitos were swarming. Wet heat radiated from the ground and from the trees. Moss commented on their discomforts with bitterness and amazement, but Thomas remained quiet, grunting occasionally so Moss wouldn't feel ignored. It was difficult work, but Thomas kept his eyes down and let his mind drift. In the hazy spaces between his slow, uninvited thoughts, the frustration of it all moved to the background.

As the day passed, they encountered more log jams. They portaged often. Sometimes the river narrowed, with tree boughs leaning over the water. There were also a series of rapids. Moss was unsure of these rapids, where the water flowed fast and with force, but Thomas called out directions. "Paddle hard!" or, "Wait!" He navigated the boat well, and a feeling of accomplishment washed over them. They had bumped into a few rocks, and there had been a sickening scrape along the bottom, but they made it through. The trees were thick, and the light no longer reached them. It was cool there, in that dark shade.

A creek flowed into the river, and when they saw it, agreed to turn in for a break. They filtered water with a pump. Mosquitos were thick here, and they found leaches on their legs from when they had lined the canoe through some debris. Blood from the leaches soaked through their pants.

"This is like a jungle," Moss muttered. "It's not fit for humans."

Thomas offered a mild assent. To live out here a person would need to move to higher ground, away from the water and mud.

"You can't even see anything more than six feet in front of you," Moss continued. "This land is not kind to people. It's one large swamp, really."

"You would have to clear bush," Thomas replied in agreement. He only spoke to be polite. He preferred not to talk. Everything was always plain as day. There was never a need for talking. Only people who didn't understand what it was all about went on gabbing like a bird.

The old map made it look like they would reach the lake that day, but as the evening approached, there was no sign of any lake. But the river opened up, flowing past an island and then expanding into gentle, rolling rapids. At the base of the rapids, they spotted a raised dry place overlooking the river. They knew this was a good place to camp.

The earth was very dry and clean here. A soft breeze blew down along the path of the river, and there were no bugs. They hardly had to speak to each other to realize this was the place to camp. Moss had the tent up quickly, and Thomas gathered firewood. Soon they had eaten and cleaned their dishes in the pebbles of the shore. They put a couple lines in the river, at the base of the rapids, and took turns sawing the firewood. As the sun settled deep behind the trees and the world became shrouded in shadow, they pulled out a plastic bottle of vodka. The world felt perfect, and they drank.

"At the bar, you drink all hunched up, wondering what time it is," Moss began. "But out here there's no rush."

"This is perfection," Thomas replied with feeling in his voice.

"Work isn't getting any easier."

Thomas said nothing to this. It pained him to think of the warehouse.

"The new boss acts like he's ready to fire someone," Moss continued.

Thomas thought of his quiet corner in the warehouse, where he had his computer. The guys would gather around him every day to look at pictures of sex. The guys understood him to be the undisputed master when it came to getting women.

"The company transfers in some bean counter from Toronto—why? Either because he sucks at his job, or they think we suck at ours." Moss looked to Thomas, wishing him to talk.

"He's harmless," Thomas replied with a shrug. Last week the boss had come by his station. Thomas had turned off his computer before the boss could see the screen. The boss was having a fit of paranoia because he was an alcoholic and didn't have friends. He was disconnected from the earth, and so needed to stay close to Thomas in order to slow the spinning of the universe. Thomas knew how to talk to the man. His instincts told him the boss was looking for a confidant, and for someone in charge. The boss didn't want to be the boss.

Thomas never did anything, really. He clicked the screen now and then when he had to clear orders from the list. He had only been at the job for three years, but he had been given the best work in the warehouse. He figured this was his right. Everything worked out for him. Especially with the ladies, he mused.

Moss wasn't sure the boss was harmless. He was scared to lose his job. He knew that sooner than later he and Alicia would be getting married. She wanted children.

"They have us on the computers now," Moss returned. "We don't get to hardly use our muscles anymore. I feel like those screens will drive me insane."

Thomas shrugged again. The boss was nuts. He had been sent north because he was unpredictable. He and the boss smoked a joint every day at lunch, out past the row of rusting shipping containers. Moss didn't know about the drugs. He always went with his lunch to a quiet corner to read. Because of this he knew no gossip, and therefore feared every little change in tone or expression that happened amongst the boys. Moss didn't realize that everyone liked him and feared him, Thomas reflected. They feared Moss because he read books. Why would a man lock himself into silence for an hour every day? What did he know? No one knew what Moss had going on in that large head of his.

"The computer drove me insane long ago," Thomas laughed. He laughed in order to relax Moss.

"That's because you're always watching crap," Moss laughed back.

Thomas returned to silence, prodding the fire with a stick. The drugs combined with the computer screen turned every afternoon into a blur of moving images, disconnected from reality. It became like a waking dream. He didn't know how to control the flow, and a part of him didn't care to learn how to control it. It just flowed and flickered, light to dark, dark to light. Over and over. He kept his earphones off, though. When sound joined the blurred images, he tended to fall to a place that he couldn't get out of until the next morning. The girls in the moving pictures were on drugs, too. He knew this in a conspiratorial way. When he was stoned he could spot a user from a mile away.

The river flowed into the night. It was luminous. It seemed to light up the whole forest. There was a quarter moon, and the stars were strewn thickly across the eternal black, but the river carried its own light. It was comforting to be able to see the river like that. It rushed loudly in the night, but this was pleasant because you could see the water frothing white. The campsite felt like the most perfect place either of them had ever come across.

The next morning, they pulled in their lines. They had two beautiful trout for breakfast. They threw the guts of the fish into the river so as not to attract bears, and put the lines back in. They looked down the river and saw more log jams. The thought of struggling with the canoe over those logs and portaging through more cedar swamp made them uneasy. Especially when they could rest like they were in this nice camp.

According to the map, there was a formal portage trail five hundred yards deeper into the woods. That afternoon they decided to reach for it, just to break the monotony of the day.

The walk into the bush turned out to be easy. There was a steady elevation, and the forest dried out. It was a pleasant walk. Soon they found the portage trail. It was grown in, and they found signs of moose.

"No one has been through here in ten years, I'd guess," said Moss.

Thomas agreed. Their map was over twenty years old. They turned and headed toward camp.

Near the river, they realized they were a hundred yards downstream. As they walked up to their camp, they came across a canoe turned neatly on its side, leaning against bush and trees. When they tried to turn it over, they saw that the bushes had grown around it so that it was tied to the spot. It was shady here, and the shiny red colouring of the canoe seemed hardly tarnished.

There was mud and leaves inside the canoe, but it was in good shape. The oars, though, were dried out and brittle.

"What's this?" asked Moss, deeply curious about the story of it.

Thomas shrugged. He loved this canoe, and decided he would take it out with them.

They paused and listened. Above the swirling gurgling of the river they could hear a bush plane. Neither man moved until they had traced the sound across the sky to its disappearance.

"The lake is probably another kilometre in," said Thomas.

"Maybe the guy who had this canoe just abandoned it and walked to the lake," offered Moss.

Thomas shrugged. Who knew? It didn't matter. The canoe was here and they had found it.

They freed the canoe and brought it to their camp.

There were two more trout on their lines, and they had a good lunch.

"Soon it will be blueberry season. I wonder if you could live out here your whole life," queried Moss aloud.

"You could," said Thomas. He felt something irritating his thoughts and feelings. At the same time, he felt something drop from beneath him, as though he were at risk of falling into a chasm. He had felt this same thing at sixteen years old, when he'd left home. His mother was an old waitress trying to be sexy, and his father was a mean drunk who lived in a trailer with a woman addicted to pills. What a strange feeling it was to realize you were alone in the world. Exhilarating and terrifying. You could do anything you wanted. The only real consequence was death, and that awaited everyone anyway. The bottom dropped out and he had allowed himself to fall. This surrender had served him well.

They napped through the afternoon. Later, they explored the island by walking across the rapids at the widest point and then swimming up in the quieter waters behind the shelter of the island. It was choked with deadfall from the spring runoff. To return to their camp, they recklessly threw themselves into the current and let the water carry them downstream to the base of the rapids. They had a few bruises from the rocks they bumped into, but they were laughing and happy over the thrill of it.

The water was cold, and it invigorated them. They ate, feeling like new men.

The vodka felt good. They agreed to return home the next morning.

"Alicia will be happy to see me," Moss said. "She was scared for us."

Thomas raised an eyebrow and looked at Moss. "Why?"

"It's dangerous out here."

"It's dangerous everywhere."

"You know what I mean," said Moss.

Thomas supposed he did know, but didn't agree. "We all die."

"I don't want to die today. I want to have babies with Alicia!" Moss exclaimed with some buffoonery, but it bothered Thomas, because he knew Moss thought of these things for real.

"There's no point," he muttered. Thomas felt uncomfortable. He became conscious that his speech was contrived, like an actor in an old western movie. He found this falseness distasteful.

"There's always a point," countered Moss. The drink was helping him feel a great love for the dry campsite and the rushing river, and for the clouds of stars twinkling and turning above them. Moss was gripped by the immense mystery of it all in that moment. He realized for the first time in his life that he had a destiny.

"I can't wait to get back to town," he finished modestly, not wanting to harm Thomas. He knew that what he was realizing was something Thomas had never come close to knowing. He knew that a man like Thomas could never experience the great love for things that he was experiencing now, without hitting rock bottom first. It wasn't fair, but it was that way anyway. Everyone had their own thing to figure out.

The next morning, when the sun cleared the trees and shone directly over the water and onto the tent, Moss woke up. The morning air was cool and fragrant with the scent of the forest. He washed his face at the river and saw Thomas sitting by the fire. He had taken the rifle out and was counting shells.

"I'm staying here," Thomas said to Moss's inquiring gaze. "You take our canoe. Leave me all the stuff with my oar, and you go back. I've got that red canoe. I'm good to go."

"What are you going to do?" asked Moss, nervousness sitting heavily in his stomach.

"I have lots of rice, fishing rods, a rifle—everything. I'm going to that lake."

Thomas added the last part in order to appease Moss. When someone thought you were going somewhere then they figured you would be fine. It was when you weren't going anywhere that people began to worry about you, or judge you.

"What about work?"

"I quit that goddamned place," Thomas said with certainty.

Moss realized that not only did he have a destiny, he also had a strength of character.

Moss gathered his few belongings that he wasn't leaving behind, and stared upriver. It would be a hard day. With his backpack on and the canoe on his shoulders, he began to work his way upstream, in the shallows.

Thomas yelled after him, "Be friends with the boss. He's helpless as a baby. You'll run that warehouse in a year!"

Moss turned and looked to Thomas from beneath the canoe. Thomas was standing with his hands in his pockets. He enjoyed watching Moss working hard, carrying that canoe like he was, in the river. Moss turned back and started walking. After a few more steps he decided to look at Thomas one last time, but he was already hidden from view by the cedar boughs that reached for the flowing waters.

Part 2: Emergence

For the record, I lived in the bush for three years, more or less. I lived on a fly-in lake. It was full of fish, like walleye and pike. I also had my rifle and a case of fifty shells. I was careful. It was easy to snare rabbits in the winter, too. You could always see their trails in the snow. The outfitter who ran the plane and the camp for American hunters knew I was on the lake, obviously. He didn't care though. He'd tip his hat to me as he boated past and just leave me alone. I never bothered his camp. I bring this up because the paper made it seem like I was living naked out there for ten years, stealing and making a nuisance of myself. I left everything alone. I never wanted for anything. I wasn't born out there and abandoned, as someone on the internet said I was. I had decided to be out there, and that's different than being abandoned. I've never been abandoned.

The outfitter did help me, though. He left lots of winter gear for me. He left it on his dock when he was closing his hunt lodge in late autumn, after the leaves had all changed and fallen. I watched him leave it too, because at the time, knowing winter was coming, I was curious about that camp and wondered whether I'd need to steal in order to survive the worst of the cold. With the winter gear was a short note that said something like, "the cabin at the point is unlocked." That's all it said. The cabin was a nice little shack with a woodstove about eight kilometers north of the lodge, and I gathered my gear and settled in there for the worst of winter. That winter gear, combined with the hunt shack, settled everything real nice. That and the big bag of rice and dried meat he'd put out. He left that food out every fall for the three winters I was out there. It made life real easy. Other than for those things, I never went near the camp.

An early memory of mine was me and three friends stealing a bottle of Coke out of the delivery truck at the corner store. We were four years old or so. We took the bottle of Coke and went and hid underneath a bush, against Tommy's house. No one could see us there. We sat in a circle with our legs crossed and passed the bottle around, burping as loudly as we could. Sometimes one of us would make the sound of sirens wailing, pretending the cops were out chasing us down for stealing. I suppose that memory sticks with me because that was the first time I remember actually doing something that was wrong.

I've never caused big trouble. I stayed quiet in school. I never got into fights or anything like that. I never dealt drugs either. I smoked weed like everyone else, but now they're making that legal anyway. Three years in the bush, though. I haven't touched a thing bad for you in three years. That changes things, I can tell you. Maybe everyone should disappear in there for three years. The world might be a better place.

It sounds funny now, maybe, but the worst moment of my life was when I was twelve. Me and Tommy had a tree house in the creek valley behind the school. We didn't build the tree house. We found it. It was probably six feet off the ground, and it had four-foot-high walls or so. Me and Tommy brought some scrap wood in there and made a type of roof, too. It had lots of holes in it. We didn't care. It was a dream. We would go in there and play pirates, and pretend our tree house was a ship. And then we'd play US Marines, and pretend we were snipers or machine gunners. It was all good in that tree house, every day, practically. We even talked of sleeping in there overnight, but we never did. We were kids, though. If our friends would have seen us playing pretend we would have been bugged about it. But it was fun being a kid.

One day we were sneaking out there, pretending to be soldiers ready to ambush a bunker, and as we snuck close to the tree house I smelled something funny. I stopped and looked over to Tommy, and his eyes lit up.

"Drugs!" he said.

What did that mean? I had no idea. I'd heard of drugs, obviously, but I didn't know anything. Were we in danger?

Tommy was so excited. He crept up on his belly while I hung back. Then he practically started rolling around, putting his fist into his mouth to stop himself from giggling. I wondered what the heck was going on, and he called me forward and showed me.

"My sister!" he says, and there were two older boys with her.

They were passing around drugs and smoking them up. Then his sister went up into the tree house with a guy, and there was all sorts of shuffling around up there, and then the one guy jumped down in a heap and the next guy climbed up. Tommy couldn't stand it. He was laughing and giggling at me quietly. The guy who had been up there first was just lying on the ground, staring up at the sky. White clouds were passing over in the summer breeze. Maybe he was looking for shapes. That's what I always did as a kid, and I did it out in the bush over those three years, on warm afternoons when food and firewood were taken care of.

I was worried, though. I was afraid of being found out, first of all. Those boys were bigger and older, and Tommy kept squirming and laughing. The other thing was, I was confused, real bad. I kept thinking that Tommy's sister needed to be rescued. And when I saw Tommy giggling like that, I couldn't help but feel he was sincerely crazy, like a devil was in him. When the second guy jumped down beside the first, my thought was that a murder had happened. How could Tommy laugh when his sister was in trouble like that?

Well, the two guys started walking all casual out of the creek valley, following one of the paths me and Tommy had made over the summer. His sister called out for them to wait, but they didn't wait, and walked on without turning around. They struck me as being like the Nazis I'd seen on TV, or maybe orcs like in *Lord of the Rings*, who only cared to fill their bellies and never worried about anything else.

Tommy's sister was struggling along after them, trying to put her clothes together. Tommy laughed and yelled out a name at her. She yelled back and threatened him. I felt queasy. I really did. I felt revulsion for Tommy and his sister. They were disgusting to me. I also felt an attraction to his sister I'd never felt about any woman before. I can tell you I never went back to that tree house ever again, and I never really played with Tommy again either. Suddenly I could remember all his jokes about sex. He was really twisted for a twelve-year-old.

That was a bad day. After that I could see that my mom dressed sexy, and that my dad was out too much. I started paying attention to the empty booze bottles, not the full ones. And I started paying attention to my mom's boyfriends. I ran away from home, if you want to use the term "runaway," sometime in my high school years. By then I realized too that the women I saw were real flesh and blood, and that there was something they had that I wanted.

So there it is. There is nothing dramatic to say about why I was in the bush. I didn't commit a murder. I didn't cross a drug dealer. I had a job at a warehouse. I mostly just sat at the computer all day. I'd go smoke up at lunch, and me and the guys would watch porn on the computer after that. I don't know how to explain it really. Why did I go off into the bush? I wanted to let everything go. That's how it was when I took off from home at sixteen. I saw nothing good. So, I figured, why not just let it all go in that case, and see where I land? Same thing with going off into the bush three years ago. Yeah, I had made money and I had bought my truck, but everything just seemed all bent out of shape. There was nothing good there, with the drinking, the drugs, and the women, so I just took a deep breath and let go. I was on a crooked path going nowhere. Why keep following it?

Living in the bush was interesting, though. I had been alone plenty of times as a kid, so being alone in the bush was not difficult. I like it. I like hearing the wind in the pines. It is just the sound of the wind, not the leaves. Sometimes I'd be out in a stand of poplar or some such tree, and the leaves would flap and crackle in the wind. That was nice too, I suppose. But the rush of wind in the pines, that is what I found most peaceful. And I didn't miss women out there, or my apartment, or my truck, and least of all my job. I sure as heck didn't miss the drugs or the booze. I had told my friend Moss, "I am heading out to the lake." He thought I was going to kill myself, probably. I've never asked him what he thought back then. I learned the authorities checked in on me when I first went missing. They asked the outfitter to contact me. Apparently, he told them I was fine, which was very true. No one else cared what I'd done.

So many things amazed me out there. One winter's night, when a blizzard brought clouds of snow across the lake and into the trees above my shack, I heard wolves howl close by. That startled me something fierce. But I took a deep breath and was okay. I heard wolves a lot around that lake. In the summer evenings, I would hear a loon call out. Sometimes I actually cried when I heard the loon. I hate to admit that in a way, but it's true. I cried. The loon is like the wolf. It has an angel's voice, if that makes sense. Far away and haunting. It touches you deep down. In my canoe, I came across a moose swimming across the lake. The moose has suffering eyes, like it is begging for mercy, and I regretted shooting it. I'll never do that again. One time a bald eagle came crashing to earth right behind me while I moved my fishing line. It slid down a pine with a lot of noise and fury. It must have pinned a bird or a squirrel.

The most amazing thing for me, though, was the silence. It would arrive in the early morning, before the light broke and the birds started to sing. That silence was deafening in a way, and it always felt to me like it was moving, filling everything that was alive or dead with a spirit or a beauty or a substance of sorts. It was in that dark, heavy silence that I realized God was there, with me. This changed me. Sometimes when that silence came I'd curl up in my sleeping bag and cover my head in fear, and sometimes I would sit up and expect to die that same moment. Usually I just lay unmoving, hoping the silence would not notice me, but would just pass. It didn't matter the time of year—the silence was always there. In the presence of the silence I became aware of how twisted my life had been. I wanted to do right by that silence.

At night, I would sit close to the fire and really take in the heat. I would stare at the blue and white coals underneath the orange flames. I could see a whole other world there, and my thoughts would just drift about, free. Sometimes I would think of my mom, who always made herself sexy for men. And I would think about her and then just say to myself, "Goodbye." And then I'd think of my dad, who just wanted to drink and fight. He could live anywhere if he had the booze. And I'd think about my dad and then say to myself, "Goodbye." And I'd go on like that with people I had known, and with bad things I had done, and I'd just say, "Goodbye." It was a good goodbye, if you know what I mean. I was out in the dark night, beside my warm fire, and I would say goodbye in a good way. I would let them be, and off they'd go, and I have never bothered to say hello to anyone since I came back out of the bush, except for the few who dropped in just to say hey. They mostly talk and talk. I don't have much to say to people I've said goodbye to.

Moss came by with his two-year-old daughter. She is a gem. I never said goodbye to Moss out there, which I find interesting. Moss is a happy man. We visited for maybe fifteen minutes and then Moss left. We didn't shake hands or anything like that. Just a hello. That was good enough. Moss wanted me to know that he loved me and was there for me. I appreciate that. I feel very good.

I suppose I do want people in my life. The hospital chaplain comes by to visit with me. That is nice. I don't think she wants to convert me or anything. I told her about the silence, and she found that interesting. She mentioned a prophet in the Bible who had the same experience of God. I thought that was cool. It made me think that maybe I'm really part of something bigger than me. I understand that there is a God, but it is difficult to talk about that with anyone. I could never tell my old friends about God, for instance. I could talk about the silence, though. With God there in the bush, on that lake, I never felt lonely.

Well, okay, I did feel lonely in the end. During the third winter out there, I realized that I didn't need to be out there anymore. That's what it was. That was when I realized not only was there a God, but that God cared for me. I had said my goodbyes, and I had fallen in love with the sky and the land and the water. I knew everything, and I knew that I no longer belonged out there. I knew I had to go back now. That was when I realized absolutely there was a God walking with me, and that I wasn't in nearly as much control of my life as I had always thought. That's because, after the silence, suddenly I felt called to return here. That probably sounds crazy, but there it is. It felt like after years of that silence, suddenly I was being spoken to in a very clear way. I also realized that most people around here think they are in control of everything. I don't find this to be funny or sad. It's just the way it is, and some people will figure this out and some won't. The end will be the same for all of us anyway. It's just you and God in the end. It makes a difference now, though, when you know you're not in control. It changes how you live. How important is that? It is important for me, is all I know. This is why I enjoyed visiting with Moses. That's his name, not Moss. Moses and I were friends before, though I don't know why. He was thoughtful and kind, and I was like an animal, but we were friends, and went on that canoe trip to the lake. We never made it, but we found a red canoe, and I went deeper into the bush, and he returned to a good life with his family. He never struck me as being off the path. He accepted the people around him, and he loved them like a man should.

Pietà

The neon light glowed warmly in the humid night. There seemed to be a physical substance to the light. It fell like a warm mist to the sidewalk. Mark felt alive in that light, and he flexed his muscles proudly. He was wearing a jean jacket so no one could see the muscles rippling from his shoulders through his arms, but he didn't care about that. He was past showing off. He was proud, because even though his youth was already spent, beneath that neon light he still had the vitality of youth in his spirit. This was most important, because there wasn't anything else that mattered in this life.

He stepped into the tavern and the air cooled. The sour smell of beer spilled long ago rose to greet him through the haze and din. There was loud chatter, and sometimes someone guffawed like a dog barking. This in turn set off a woman's laughter, which was shrill and drunk.

The stage overlooking the dance floor was set up with a drum kit and microphones. There were also two stools and a pitcher of beer with empty glasses. The blues band was from Tennessee. In Canada, it was easy to romanticize about a blues band from there, or Alabama, or Louisiana.

Through the first set, Mark and Rolly drank two pitchers of beer. There was nothing to talk about. Twice, acquaintances from the bar sat at their table. They shook hands. But it was hard to talk above the music, and there wasn't anything really going on that could have kept a conversation going. Mark knew this, as did the others. He had to restrain himself from bringing up the Maple Leafs. Such contrived conversation would have been foolish. But Mark wanted to talk about something. In the end, it was easier to just drink beer.

As the first set was close to wrapping, a young girl leapt ecstatically to the stage. Mostly older couples in jeans and leather vests danced, but now this young thing with tassels on her sequined jacket came before the band and gyrated and jumped in rhythm to the music. The lead singer looked over to the bassist and shook his head with an ironic smile. It was a subtle acknowledgment, though. The singer really was cool, and exuded laid-back confidence, as though everything would be alright for everyone. Mark could tell that the singer was more worried about the girl than anything else. The girl was really making a spectacle of herself, jumping around crazily without ever slowing down, and Rolly began to appraise her carefully. Maybe he would have to go and say hello. As the last song of the set ended, the girl turned and ran out the back of the tavern and into the alley, holding her mouth. This caused Rolly to bark out a short laugh. Mark didn't want to get caught up in it, and intentionally began to think of work at the warehouse. He wondered if his boss was also on the take. They were receiving more dope from Montreal every week.

As the chatter resumed, Mark noticed two young guys at the bar. They were talking to Jumping Joe, one of the bouncers. J. J. was almost six-and-a-half feet tall, and three hundred pounds. He drove a Harley, but he wasn't in a biker gang. He was mostly a poser, actually. No one wanted to fight him after sizing him up, and whenever J. J. found himself in a tussle, the other bouncers were always there to help. He liked being everyone's friend, and he liked the status that came with bouncing at the crumbling down blues bar. J. J. pointed the young men in the direction of Mark and Rolly, and they came over and stood awkwardly.

"Hash?" one asked.

"You selling?" Rolly chirped back. Rolly was sharp-witted, and never hesitated when violence threatened in a meeting between men.

One of the young men couldn't stand the tension, and rolled his shoulders away from the table. He went and stood near the bar, staring off at the empty stage.

"Buying," said the other.

Rolly turned and looked to Mark, ignoring the man. "Should we get a smoke?"

They got up and went out the back. Rolly gave a slight nod to the man and he followed. The uncomfortable one trailed far behind, hesitating.

The young girl called for them to keep the exit door open. She was leaning up against a brick wall, the tassels on her coat swinging back and forth as she rocked on the balls of her feet. The band also came out, each with a glass of beer and a smoke. Everyone greeted each other and shook hands while the girl leaned down onto her knees. She wasn't dancing anymore, that was for sure. It smelled of vomit when a breeze drifted through the alleyway. Rolly glanced in her direction and laughed, rolling his eyes with amusement.

The young guy wanting the hash wasn't sure what to do. He didn't even have a drink. He hadn't seen the set either. He just wanted drugs.

"How's Tennessee?" Mark asked the lead singer.

"Fine, fine. Always good people in Tennessee," he replied, taking a deep drag.

"You guys want some hash?" Rolly asked. "On the house."

"Is he a cop?" the singer laughed, taking a drink while jabbing a smoke at the young guy.

"He's a nothing," Rolly answered matter-of-factly. Just then, the young guy's timid partner pushed open the door, causing everyone to turn and look. Everyone laughed. He came through the door and stood beside his friend, looking at the ground.

"How much do you want?" Rolly asked the young guy now, condescendingly.

They made a deal, and the young guy said thanks. They left down the alley, passing the girl without even looking at her.

Mark and Rolly lit up and smoked together with the band. They all laughed, talking about border guards in white shirts and ties who acted macho.

"Some people devote themselves to the image of something," mused the singer. "They don't live in the spirit." He gazed up to the night sky. It was hard to see any stars, for there were clouds drifting through, and the city's light reflected off of them.

"The spirit?" asked Rolly. "Are you religious?" He didn't ask this with any judgment. He just wanted to know the substance of the man.

"I suppose I am," said the bluesman with a smile forming on one corner of his mouth. "I'm talking about the spirit of life. Who wants to play a role? Be real is all I'm saying."

"Hey man, different strokes for different folks," returned Rolly with a shrug. It meant nothing to him what a man believed, or how a man saw himself.

Feeling quite high, Mark began to think he was part of something serious and real. At the same time, and with some admiration and jealousy, he considered Rolly to be utterly devoid of a self-conscious thought. Rolly just did what the moment before him called for.

The night was full of possibilities, as was every night. Rolly gave a ball of tinfoil full of hash to the singer and wished him well on his travels.

"Welcome to Canada," he said as they shook hands goodbye.

Mark noticed the girl was still resting there. The earth kept spinning, and she couldn't stop it. She would end up sleeping in that alley, he thought. Why didn't anyone come out to help her? Why was she alone and lost? He wanted to pick her up and take her home. He wanted to help her, because she was so badly drunk. Perhaps they'd become friends and start dating. Maybe they'd even get married. She was very beautiful, that much anyone could tell.

His car was around the corner. Rolly wanted a ride home even though the night was still young. The doors creaked and slammed shut heavily. Mark was proud of his car. It was a well-kept, '78 Chrysler Newport. It bounced when they drove over dips in the road. Mark had bought the car from a war vet and had put a CD player in himself. He dreamed the car would help him meet people, but mostly people were more scared of him than before, because now he really looked like a gangster.

"I have a job in the morning," Rolly said, lighting another smoke. "Do you want to come along? I'll pay you a thousand bucks."

The Rolling Stones were playing on the stereo.

"What are you doing for a thousand bucks?" Mark asked. That was a week's pay at the warehouse.

"The job is for three grand. Out of the goodness of my heart, I want to pay you a grand."

Mark cursed his approval.

"It's for our guy. I just have to pick up a package for him at a hotel. He's dealing with new people. It'd be good if you were there, like for backup."

Mark lit up a smoke because it seemed like the right thing to do. In the movies, that's what they'd do.

He and Rolly had been through a lot together. They'd played hockey on the junior team. It was a glorious thing, looking back. They'd wreaked havoc with their teammates drinking, smoking up, and picking up women. Fighting together, partying together, and playing the game. Everyone together like a gang of brothers. He had felt invincible.

The streetlamps were in the middle of the trees. In the dark night fumes of the city, the streetlamps lit up the boulevard and cast it in shadow all at the same time. "Gimme Shelter" by the Stones was playing now, and the cool air rushed over the skin of his arm and made his long hair tug and flow like a horse's mane. He felt like a god, at one with the dark and lonely city. He also felt alone, with no one to share the wonders of it all.

He ached for what had been, and agreed to go with Rolly.

The next morning at eight-thirty, Rolly swung by in his old pickup truck. Mark jumped in, carrying a coffee. He'd had a lousy sleep.

They sped off to the outskirts of town without a word shared between them, and turned into a buckling and weed-infested parking lot of a motel. It was called the Roadrunner Motor Motel. It had seen better days. Hardly anyone was staying there. A real dive. The large neon sign at the front was rusting, and you could see the broken bulbs. A picture of a roadrunner in a convertible was faded, with a blotch of rust right in the middle of it.

Rolly stopped the truck in the middle of the lot for a moment and reached over Mark's lap to the glove box. He pulled out a .38, along with a heavy brown envelope.

"What in the hell are you going to do with a gun?" Mark asked, keeping his voice casual.

"Nothing. Just extra backup."

Mark could see that Rolly's hands were shaking.

"I thought I was the backup."

Rolly smiled painfully. He was so tight that he couldn't really smile at all. He drove up to a room and parked beside an old navy blue Delta '88.

"That car looks like your piece of crap," Rolly muttered.

Mark snickered. He was feeling nervous now too, because he'd never seen Rolly nervous about anything.

Rolly looked ridiculous putting the .38 in his pants like a guy would in the movies, but Mark didn't say anything. He didn't want to provoke his nervous friend.

They went up to the door. It was orange, with a black 16 painted on it.

A man with thin blond hair and a mustache opened it for them. He had on a black tee-shirt. He had muscles and looked tough, but Mark knew that he could take him if it came to that. From the light of the doorway Mark could also see a balding man in a short-sleeved button-down shirt. He stood near the bathroom at the back. He was a heavyset man, and had a cunning look to his eyes. It was his eyes that made Mark fear a fight with him. Some people never gave up in a fight until someone was dead.

Rolly offered a friendly greeting. His enthusiasm wasn't matched by the men. As Mark entered the room, he saw the TV was on. There were two young girls in their panties, wearing matching white tee-shirts, watching from the nearest bed. Mark saw they were watching Bugs Bunny cartoons. He slid over till he was standing beside the girls. He knew this cartoon. It was Bugs Bunny visiting a haunted house.

"Abracadabra!" said Bugs Bunny. The ghostly vampire stalking him was changed to a bat.

Mark looked to the girls with a smile on his face. He had loved that cartoon as a kid. The girls didn't laugh or even smile. They didn't even return his look. They just stared at the TV with vacant eyes. They were hungover from meth maybe, or just hash and booze.

He looked up to see Rolly talking to the big man with cunning eyes. The blond was behind Rolly. It was small talk. They wanted to know more about the guy Rolly was working for. He still held the brown envelope in his hand, propped against his leg.

Bugs Bunny was still learning about the power of magic. Mark smiled again and looked to the girls.

"I like this one," he said to them. The one closest to him turned and looked him in the eye. She smiled.

"It's funny," she said. She turned back to the TV.

"Are you from around here?" Mark asked.

"Sort of," the girl said, still looking at the TV. "We get moved around," she continued when Mark kept looking at her.

She was very beautiful, with large brown eyes, but she and her friend were very young. He guessed them to be fifteen. Mark felt sick to his stomach, seeing them there like that with two gangsters. It was all wrong.

"Who moves you?" he prodded. He couldn't take his eyes off her. She was like an angel.

"Her brother," she said, nodding to her friend.

Mark thought he could see the girl clearly. She had no idea about anything being right or wrong.

Still, he couldn't help himself. "Do you want help?"

"What are you, Mother Teresa?" asked the blond man to Mark. He laughed, looking Mark up and down.

Bugs Bunny was really in the swing of things now. He was having his way with the ghoulish vampire, and the girl laughed out loud. Mark thought this was an improvement on things. At least she wasn't just zoned out.

The guys had all lit up, and the girl looked to Mark and asked for a smoke. Her partner just sat there, staring at the TV. He offered her one. She leaned over and let him light it for her. A gold crucifix on a chain slipped out from under the tee-shirt. He remembered crisp white altar cloths and albs, and sprinkles of holy water on his face. He remembered the scent of beeswax candles and incense. He thought of the pietà he had stared at as an altar boy every time he went into the sanctuary to robe up. The blood on Jesus's face, the wound in his side, and the mournful look of the Virgin as she implored the heavens for a different ending to things.

"Are you Christian?" Mark asked the girl.

The blond man thought this was so hilarious that he had to tell Rolly and his partner.

"I have a guardian angel," the girl said, looking to Mark with pride in her eyes.

They were all laughing now, but the pride the girl felt for her guardian angel made her set her jaw firmly. Mark realized she did know right from wrong. The girl knew she was trapped, but she had something else too, something that could always remind her about her.

Mark could feel his lungs empty as he exhaled slowly. He didn't have anything.

"You're such a tool," Rolly said to Mark. The gangsters thought Rolly was okay, and they laughed again.

Mark said, "See you," to the girl, and went to the door, his shoulders sagging. Rolly followed him out.

Driving back, Rolly was ecstatic. "This business is going to work out fine," he said.

Mark watched the city beneath the light of the sun. It was turning into a hot day. He didn't know if he should go to the bar and drink all day, or just take a walk down by the river and never stop. Just keep walking, right out of the city. Rolly was talking, but Mark couldn't hear him. There were just roads and cars and businesses and billboards. That gasping, mournful beseeching of the Virgin was the most truthful thing he'd ever come across, for sure. He looked forward to the night.

The Intellectual

He sat at his desk and wrote a poem. It was a very good poem. It was seven lines long and was about a woman and their shared love. He knew the woman too. She was a petite redhead who lived a few blocks over. They had said hello to each other on three occasions. Each time she had walked down the street while he was sitting outside on an old lawn chair that was ready to fall apart, resting beneath the shade of an equally old patio umbrella he had stuck into the dirt of his failing front lawn. He supposed it was quicker for her to cut by on his street toward her house, though maybe she had walked by his place on purpose because she liked him. She lived in a small, square bungalow with a blue pyramid roof. It was very quaint.

In his poem their love was whispered, but it was a deeply sad love because they would never be able to consummate it. The sufferings of life were pulling them apart. Life is full of suffering, he thought, and gazed over his books with a melancholy that he felt was actually quite pleasing, in a fatalistic way.

The first time she had walked by, he had first heard her heels clicking on the pavement. He had been sitting back and smoking a joint while contemplating the beauty of an untended yard. His grandpa, who had lived in the house for fifty years, had always kept the lawn perfectly trimmed. A weed wouldn't have dared to show itself around him. With a laugh, he thought how his own philosophy about front yards differed from his grandpa's. Let it all run amok, he thought happily. If anything will break down the divide between rich and poor, it will be the destruction of the front yard as an aesthetic. There was a stand of sunflowers at the corner of his front yard, however, planted by the kind old lady he had as a neighbour. She was an old Italian woman from another time, and had known his grandpa and grandma. She thought she was doing him a favour, and he had to admit he liked those tall flowers. They seemed almost sentient, and he would observe their large faces carefully most sunny afternoons after the joint had been smoked.

As it was, the sunflowers obscured his vision down the sidewalk, so, as the clicking heels neared, he inhaled deeply from the joint as though the dope had visionary qualities, and he tried to imagine what kind of woman belonged to those heels. As she passed by, she looked up and saw him. She smiled an unspoken, gentle hello. He had quickly sat up straight, giving a guarded smile while slowly releasing the smoke from his lungs. He felt ridiculous as the smoke wafted gently from the sides of his smiling mouth, like a dragon sidekick who always screwed up.

She wore a light summer dress, and he had fallen in love immediately. But he was worried about the ganja. What if she frowned upon drug use? As her gaze turned back to the sidewalk, it seemed her smile slid from one of open hello to ironic judgment, but he couldn't be sure. In that moment, he also grew self-conscious of his ridiculous yard with its patches of dirt and weeds, with his rotting lawn chair, and his tee-shirt advertising the movie *Blade Runner*. He was vaguely aware of the fact that until that moment of meeting the beauty in the sundress, he had been quite proud of the tee-shirt. The movie was literary and esoteric, and most mindless consumers out there hadn't seen it, which enhanced his soulful groove of mystery and intelligence that separated him from the herd. Now, with the beauty's gaze upon him, the shirt suddenly felt like a declaration of juvenility.

It was a wonderfully warm evening. He put five cans of craft beer in a canvas bag and walked over to the party. He passed the church and looked up at the steeple. He felt liberated. He had his meditations. He didn't need anybody or anything, and that was a great feeling.

41

The house was packed with people. There was a keg, and the drink was flowing. Music played loudly; Thump! Thump! Thump! Friends were at the back door and in the yard, so he stood with them and drank beer. The canvas sack was tied to his belt so that the beer could be guarded. Some Gollum was always sneaking around looking for free booze.

The first four beers flowed down his throat quite easily. Times were changing. Some friends were going to be leaving the city in September. All the good times hung in the balance. The gatherings at the café, the movies they'd watched at the film society, and the late-night strolls down the boulevard—all of it now revealed as transient, as building blocks for a project that would never be properly finished. All of it was becoming something of the past. Even this party. Why did things like friendship have to change or disappear? Why couldn't friends just stay together?

What would he do in September? He'd begin his sixth year of doctoral studies at the university, of course, finishing his thesis, a Marxian analysis entitled *There Is No Eternity*, a survey of civilizational power structures that controlled the masses. He would also keep waiting tables at the New York Empire, an American chain of family steak houses. He considered this work to be revolutionary activity, since he couldn't think of a better way to trivialize and undermine capitalist culture than to wear the Empire State Building hat management made him wear while serving "Big Apple Burgers" and "Times Square Sirloins" to hungry and stressed families. Beyond these anchors in his life, he would continue writing, and looking for roles to play in the community theatre. But the evenings at home were long. They were long now, even with his friends around.

The fifth beer was the most gratifying. It drove the sad wonderings of a summer's evening away. Then a friend put a plastic cup in his hand, filled at the keg. He was feeling invincible now, and a vision came to him. His poetry and short stories would be published, and his publisher would find cafés around Toronto where he would read to the people. He pulled out a smoke and lit up. A cigarette was such a beautiful thing when you'd had a few drinks. Smoking dope was for the afternoons, when you had to write poetry or pass the time.

Besides that, things would happen. He'd meet a girl for instance, and start going out every evening. He would find the courage to talk to the petite redhead. Too bad she wasn't at the party. Now was the time, to be sure. Besides that, maybe he'd join some sort of group, like a community association to end homelessness, or a literary club at the library, even though most of the readers and writers there were older moms and retirees. They wouldn't understand his words, that was for certain.

With his beer gone, he accepted a micky of whiskey from a pal. It still had three swigs left in it.

"Thanks man," he said with brotherly affection. They were all brothers, but they were all going their own way. Some had a girl taking them away, some had visions of education and careers, and some had a cousin or a friend who could get them work in construction with good money and a cool house to live in. There were great parties to be found out in the smaller towns and cities, he was told. There was nature to explore, and less pollution and congestion. It was cheaper to live outside the city, he was reminded whenever he grew cynical about their leaving. His friends who were single were especially possessed by wanderlust. Not him, though. This was the place. Why move somewhere else to feel the same dissatisfactions and experience the same sufferings as he felt here? He felt pretty goddamned wise, and began a loud oratory on the illusions all around them in this consumeristic, tech age.

"One day our society will be enlightened," he proclaimed. He felt like saying, "follow me," but knew better. Still, one of his friends guffawed.

"Enlightened, my ass," the friend snickered. They almost came to blows as they argued for and against the evolutionary progress of civilization, but in the end, he didn't even believe himself, and was furious for orating at all, only so that a dumbass who didn't read could come across as smarter than him.

He went back into the house where things remained very crowded and loud. He got a new plastic cup of beer from the keg as two police officers appeared at the door. The party was too noisy. He shot the cops a dirty look, and then the cops left and he felt pretty good. He ended up meeting a brunette with red lipstick, and they visited about the things they did to amuse themselves in their free time. She was impressed that he wrote poetry. They had to yell in order to be heard over the music, but this also brought them closer together, and he felt shivers when her hot, sweet breath rushed past his ear. People kept drifting in and out, and at some point he became separated from the brunette. That was okay, he supposed. He wasn't sure what would have happened anyway, but he always hated the complications that came the day after a party, especially with people whose names he didn't even know.

It was two in the morning, and pretty much time to leave the party. Then the girl with the red lipstick was back, and she smiled widely with those red lips, and he began to see something sinister and mocking. Her laughing lips suggested that she knew something he didn't, and that maybe she was the master of this whole scene. What was this? What was happening? He mumbled something even he didn't understand, and waved to her as though he'd be back in an instant, and he was out of there, onto the sidewalk. He felt like he was sneaking away, which he was. He threw his cup of beer into a tall shrub and began walking home. He looked carefully at the sidewalk to make sure he walked in a straight line.

The hush and rush of traffic a few blocks over on the boulevard wove its way through the tall trees. He found this gentle, distant sound to be comforting, like the sounds of a river, and he grew romantic. People, all belonging to his tribe, were out and about. He was not alone. He was surrounded intimately by a community of people, and they were all in it together.

He stared down the sidewalk, searching for its end. It stretched into shadow far ahead, following a straight line. It was time itself. He was walking along the passing of time. Illusions and attachments beckoned from either side—rabbit trails leading off into a maze of enslavements. He followed the straight line of time. If he stayed on this path, he could maintain his freedom. Everything was going to be alright, but he felt alone and lonely, and couldn't wait to get home and fall asleep.

Farther along he saw footprints embedded in the sidewalk. Thirty years earlier, when the cement had been freshly poured, some punk had decided to have some fun and had taken a short walk, leaving their prints in the sidewalk forever. People feared non-existence, he mused. He thought of the prehistoric, fossilized footprints left somewhere in Africa, made in freshly fallen volcanic ash. He had come across the image of these footprints in a magazine article in the doctor's office. The million-year-old footprints revealed two little people, four-and-a-half feet high, walking away from the volcano. Perhaps they had been holding hands as they walked. They probably couldn't even speak to each other with a developed language, but they had understood the volcano and were walking away from it. Maybe there was nothing fearful or sad about their walk together. Maybe the warm ash felt good on their bare feet, and maybe they delighted in playing and dancing in the ash as it drifted back to earth.

Whatever it was, they were dead and gone now. He remembered them because of their fossilized footprints. By remembering them, was he praying for them? Had they found happiness? Had the world made sense a million years ago? Were there things to fear then, or was everything accepted for what it was? Had they been free of illusions? He suspected those two little hominids a million years ago probably did live without illusions. They saw things as they were, and death was simply one more thing that was easily accepted because it was part of this world of suffering.

He arrived at the avenue with the church. The streets were all deserted, and shadows lay about under the trees. The streetlamps hummed gently in the air. Moths flew in tight circles around the light, never satisfied that they were close enough.

He turned left, thinking he'd cut through a park. It was scary walking through a city park at night.

They weren't well lit, but it was good to acknowledge fears and to face them. Overcoming fears cut through a lot of nonsense and brought a person back to reality, he thought. He grew excited by the words that had just flitted through the haze of his fatigued mind. *I need to write this down before I forget*, he thought wildly. Someone in a café would read his words, and people would thank him for bringing the human race along on the passing of time. With that, the words were promptly jumbled and rearranged in his head, and he couldn't remember the original meaning. Well, tomorrow when he sat to write it would all come back to him.

There was a police car ahead, parked by the road, its lights blinking red and blue. He didn't cross the road, but stayed under the trees along a narrow sidewalk. As he approached, he saw yellow police tape everywhere, and then the yellow tape blocked him from crossing the street. He would have to move along a block and cross over at the church. That was okay. Something serious had happened here. Then, looking beyond the yellow tape, he saw a shoe on the avenue, and a trail of blood. The blood gleamed in the light of the streetlamps. Everything was fresh and undisturbed. He paused before the blood and lit a cigarette.

A girl of maybe eighteen appeared from between the hedges behind him.

"My uncle was hit by a truck," she said with a small voice.

"Oh, really?" he asked, dumbfounded. What should he say?

"He was going for some smokes down at the store," she continued, nodding down the block to the convenience store with its lit-up sign. "A truck just came ripping up the road and ran right over him," she finished, looking into his eyes for a moment as if inviting him to make sense of this for her.

"That sucks," he began, and stopped. What a stupid thing to say. "Would you like a smoke?"

She accepted, and he held out his lighter.

"Did they catch the driver of the truck?" he asked.

"Yes—it was a young guy." She inhaled deeply.

He inhaled, too, holding the smoke in so he wouldn't have to talk. There wasn't much to say, he concluded, exhaling with resignation, though he felt great affection for the girl.

"One minute everything's fine, and the next everything's different," he philosophized.

She understood this, and nodded to him. "Yes, you have to count your blessings all the time, because one day it's just over. I hope my uncle will be okay." She gripped her elbows, embracing herself tightly as she shivered. The night was getting cold.

"He's alive?" he asked. This took away some of the tension as far as he was concerned, and his tongue-tied confusion only grew.

"I don't know," she replied. "He wasn't in good shape."

He really wanted to know if the uncle was dead or alive. To be dead was easy to understand. But what did it mean if the uncle was now going to lie in a hospital for a year, maybe even attached to a machine just to stay alive? How could that be comprehended? What kind of existence was in store for him? Maybe it'd be better to just be plain dead, he thought. End of story.

He didn't want to leave her side. He wondered if she could be his girlfriend. Gazing at her upturned face, he thought she wanted a hug and maybe a kiss, but even as he leaned down toward her he realized she was gazing past him to the steeple that overlooked this scene. He turned to look at it too.

"I can only hope and pray," she said.

"Yeah, that's right," he replied. But as he said so, he realized that he most certainly did not believe in prayer. But how could he explain to her about meditation and illusions, the unconscious mind, and enlightenment? If they became lovers then they could support one another through times like these, but as he gazed at her face it was obvious that she really did care for her uncle, and that she wasn't just acting like she was in a movie, and that maybe her prayers would be real and from her heart. She didn't need his body. Just his prayers, or his spirit, or his presence on a dark night when someone who was loved had been violently injured.

"It's a bad way to end a Saturday night," he said to her, and turned back to the shoe, and to the blood that still gleamed there on the avenue.

"Yes," she began. She felt a deep despair for her uncle. He was always joking and looking on the bright side of things. And then just like that, his warm, happy presence was gone. All those family evenings around the table playing cards or crokinole, and all those summer gatherings around the back-yard fire. Her uncle was a pillar for the family, and now he was gone. It would leave a hole in the family. She looked back at the steeple.

"He will always watch over us," she said, fearing the worst.

"Yes, for sure," he nodded, cringing at how contrived that idea was.

She had been the first to come to his uncle's side as he lay unmoving on the road. It was hard to admit, but she was pretty sure she had seen parts of his brain. She believed that he would watch over them all. She could feel his presence with her even now. This presence gave her perspective, a broader vision, and suddenly she understood that the man beside her with the cigarettes was probably more interested in her body than her heart. Given the circumstances, this disgusted her, but she brushed aside the distaste she felt for the man who continued to gaze out over the accident scene without expression. He was someone to avoid, but there was no need to make a fragile man feel bad about himself. Life was tough enough without self-loathing added to the mix. She knew this from personal experience.

He observed the girl casually from the corner of his eye, and heard her talk about her uncle watching over them. She was thinking about others, the family, and suddenly he felt distaste for the girl. She was not alone. She was part of a group with a shared story. There were loyalties there in the family, and love, and there was protection from the sufferings of reality. He figured the girl wasn't really speaking to him, and he felt disconnected from all of this.

He said goodbye, and continued his walk home. This is the kind of thing for a poem or a story, he thought. He figured tomorrow he'd go to the secondhand bookstore with the café and maybe order a strong coffee, and write. It felt good to write, and he hoped someday someone would read his writing, because it really was good.

Happiness

She cleaned up breakfast with a feeling of over-whelming contentment. The counters were granite, solid and rooted in a spacious, freshly reno-vated house. She felt like she owned the foundation of all things. "Were you there in the beginning, when I created all you see?" God had asked Job. *Indeed, I think I was there*, she thought to herself. If she would have allowed it, at that moment her smile would have widened into one of utter rapture.

Her husband had just left on another trip. He was a hard-assed lawyer who took no crap, no sir—a man's man—an international traveller, and a hunter and golfer on days off. She was proud of him. People were either intimidated by him or wanted to be his friend.

She did the laundry with that same self-satisfied smile. Laundry was enjoyable in the well-lit room with the state-of-the-art machines, because she chose to do laundry. Some poor immigrant woman could be hired to clean the house and do the laundry, but this was better. Keep a handle on the money, keep outsiders out, and keep moving. To cease moving was to die. Sharks never slept.

She skimmed through the news on Facebook, stopping to chat with a few teachers and superintendents who weren't able to retire yet like she had done the year before. Through gossip and innuendo, they were able to take down a principal and a few families whose kids were totally off the rails. In the end, people on Facebook expressed their desire to be like her. No surprise there.

With a glance at the family portraits, she returned to the kitchen for another cup of tea.

She would garden that morning and work out in the afternoon. She loved her body, and she loved treating it well.

"I am a temple. I will honour my temple," she said in a whisper. This was a mantra she had fallen into the habit of repeating whenever she needed to ground herself. God, she loved her body!

Outside, there was the sound of brakes screeching. The neighbours across the street. They were a pain in the ass. Why did they even live here, in this part of town? This neighbourhood was not for them. They let their dandelions grow. In this town, people were always finding themselves in the wrong place. Not like Toronto or Ottawa. She and her husband agreed that, in a year, they'd live part-time in Toronto. They were well set up there, and political opportunities were also showing themselves. His work contacts combined with her work in the Ministry of Education had made all of this inevitable. They'd be closer to the children this way, too.

The rusted truck belonging to the neighbours was parked in front of her house. What the hell was that all about? It had a trailer attached, with a dented fishing boat. Why did some people make fishing look like an inbred activity fit for Neanderthals? Honestly. Banjo playing, backcountry hicks. The father over there was always covered in dirt while tinkering on some goddamned thing, and the mother was always with a kid in arms. The mother wore a sort of contented smile that really pissed her off. The mother thought she had it all. God almighty! The mother would hold the infant child and shoo along the other two brats while keeping track of the mongrel dog that yelped away every night.

Idiot mutt. She and her husband had joked a few times about getting the hunting rifle and just ending that joke bastard of a canine.

In the afternoon, she'd have to go work out. Would the truck still be there? The front of the truck was about a foot into her driveway. The nerve! Honest to God, how could people live with such a lack of mindfulness? She breathed deeply to remind herself about her own training in mindfulness. Feeling centred, she went to her phone and called for the town bylaw officer. He was a clown, but obviously useful.

In the garden, everything looked very nice. The carrots, the beets, the kale, and the herbs were all strong and healthy. She collected some lemon and mint leaves for a nice tea. She watered the garden with a gentle spray. The grass was soft and thick beneath her sandaled feet. A robin hopped along, looking for a worm, and she paused with the watering in order to watch the bird. It was all very beautiful. The air was clean and fresh, and bees buzzed lazily along the flowered hedge. Soon the raspberries would begin to ripen. It felt like the garden of Eden. *I am safe*, she thought.

She heard a vehicle stop on the street out front. She crept to the corner of the house and peered through a cedar bush as the bylaw officer began to write up a ticket on the truck. Hmm. She felt a prick in her conscience. Should she have phoned? There was still plenty of room to negotiate when backing out of the driveway. The truck wasn't really in the way at all. Her Mercedes had a back-up camera, proximity warning systems, and even automated steering and braking. Any drooling blockhead could back that car out of the driveway.

Too late now, but she worried. It wasn't very neighbourly. At the right time, she would have to feign surprise over the bylaw officer's presence to let the neighbours know that what was happening was news to her.

The father came out, the rickety screen door slamming behind him, and walked over to the bylaw officer with a humble gait. The father was trying to say everything was okay and that he'd move the truck. The bylaw officer, round like an apple and used to abuse, stubbornly shook his large head. He hardly had a neck.

The father's face darkened. "What the hell, man?"

The mother came out. The mother had an anxious look on her face, biting her lower lip.

That's more like it, she thought, still hiding out behind the cedar. This was becoming immensely gratifying.

The father turned on the mother and yelled at her. The mother had a stunned look on her face, and yelled back defensively, "I'm sorry! I'm sorry!" The father muttered something else at her that couldn't be heard from the cedar bush. The two of them gazed across the street at their truck and boat, at the bylaw officer, and to her house. Luckily, she was well hidden behind the cedar.

Evidently, the mother had been driving the truck, and had made a huge mistake. *Her mistake was to brush up to close to me*, she thought. *I put her back where she belongs. Now maybe they'll begin to understand where they fit in—in the grand scheme of things, that is.*

She retreated around the back of her house and entered through the sliding door. The mongrel

57

barked and the father yelled once more. A child was crying. Complete chaos was descending on that household. She could still hear the noise from the kitchen. She found that the noise was growing into a distraction from the pleasure she was feeling.

In the kitchen was a pantry. It was dark and cool. She went into the pantry, choosing not to turn on the light. Now everything felt very quiet and very perfect. She could feel the cold stone tiles with her bare feet. The stone floor had been expensive, but her husband had only shrugged at the cost. They had more money than they knew what to do with, anyway. And he liked quality, just like she did.

Now she heard the muffled bang of the truck door slamming shut, and the engine racing as the truck, and presumably the boat, went speeding off down the road. The father would probably get a speeding ticket, or wreck the boat in the blind rage that now possessed him. The mother would probably yell at the kids, or decide not to play with them today. Like a wrecking ball! And the bylaw officer clown, that fat tub of lard. He was probably really loving his job right about now.

Staring at a jar of light peanut butter on the shelf before her, she allowed her rapturous smile to spread cheekbone to perfect cheekbone.

"Don't mess with me!" she whispered. Oh God, she felt so good.

Death in Schumacher

was thirteen when I saw the reality of death. Death is the supreme form of being alone, unless your Maker happens to be with you, of course, but that possibility is unquantifiable. All we can do is bear witness to the fact before us. Feelings on the matter are relevant only to the person who is actually feeling. The dying have their own journey, a journey that at times looks like a birthing, a pilgrimage to something beyond the banalities we live within daily. I have to remind myself that one day I will die.

I was in Schumacher one summer evening, running around with three or four friends, including my friend Paul. We were doing nothing but poking fun and laughing with each other, trading humorous barbs with eight-year-olds who were pestering us on their bikes. In a moment of pure joy, I pushed one of the kids from his bike, and started cycling around in circles with it, like a way gone fool. As the kid began to chase me, off I went!

I pedalled down the bumpy and cracked street, past houses with open front doors. In the shadows of the doorways I saw old people stooped on chairs, enjoying the warm-cool drafts of a summer evening after the heat of the day. I saw working men with children at their feet, drinking beer with a hose in hand, watering their petite checkerboard front yards, wondering how they had landed where they were. Once upon a time, these same men streamed like ants from the McIntyre mine at shift change. They went straight into the hotel taverns before continuing on home with an arm over a friend's shoulder, laughing with a happy buzz beneath the headframe and the church steeple. Now they drove home from the warehouse or the machine shop further out in Timmins or Porcupine, alone in their work, and alone with their families.

I biked past the run-down drug houses where music played, aggressively loud, drunken shouts emanating from dark and smoky innards like the howling of beasts. I flew past all these places, and they disappeared from my life. I was a comet, clear and free.

I yelled and whooped and made the sound of sirens, and I picked up speed and felt the rush of air on my bare arms, goose bumps appearing, the wind blowing through my hair, my tee-shirt flapping like a flag at sea, my friends running behind me laughing and shouting "Faster! Faster!" as I pedalled harder, not wanting to ever stop.

I heard the rumble of distant thunder growl from darkly laden clouds on the far-reaching western horizon. They sat heavily there, like the end of time or the edge of the world, or like an oppressive castle wall separating us from something eternally beyond; but the clouds were too far away for a boy on a bike to think that the rain would ever come in this lifetime. I sailed with great speed past the corner store, the smell of garbage filling the air all around it, and past tables and lamps and mildewed couches and mattresses that had seen grander days. All of this waste resting on the streets, refuse set free by landlords whose evicted tenants had avoided three months' rent by making a run for it.

I pedalled madly down the main street like a runaway train, leaving my friends far behind and joyously panting for breath, a shout of protest following me for a moment from the boy whose bike I had hijacked. I was free, and I pedalled and pedalled and almost began crying with the exhilaration of it all as I passed through the airy blue light of dusk.

After a couple blocks, my legs grew fatigued, and I slowed the wheels of the bike. I turned up a street onto a hill, and I had to get off the too-small bike and walk alone and silent, my freedom robbed from me in an instant. The robbery, the thievery! Not only was my freedom taken from me suddenly, it was taken with a stubbornness and a presence—gravity, of course—that was so beyond my powers to resist that I couldn't even remember the fleeting freedom of grace I'd enjoyed only seconds earlier. I became deflated and forlorn.

Once more, I was revisited by a familiar weight called aloneness. I didn't see my aloneness as unique to me—I saw it as a universal, hulking presence affecting everyone, like a disinterested God, or a conniving demon intent on extinguishing the little sparks that still glowed in a boy's heart. I despised the aloneness, even though I was surrounded by friends. In fact, the presence of my friends made it worse, because they made me wonder what really connected us to each other, anyway. Our friendships could end with a snap of the fingers over a misconceived sleight, or plain jealousy.

I walked beneath all those crazy, fence-like, overhead wires that latticed the skies of Schumacher, not looking forward to seeing my friends again, but knowing there was nowhere else to go. I got back on the bike, the seat now uncomfortable, and pedalled back to the junction at the school. My friends, followed by the boy, walked up to greet me, all of them laughing over the boy's protests. Children screamed with unfettered delight in the nearby playground, and I grew angry.

I was about to throw the bike roughly to the ground, but in the end, seeing the pleading eyes of the boy in his ridiculous, too-big bike helmet, I handed him the bike gently, moving it ever so slightly from the outstretched hands of a friend. I thanked the boy for the ride and took a deep breath to calm myself, as I received a friendly slap on the shoulder. Night was coming, so we began to disperse, me going to Paul's house for root beer. We were wistful and melancholy, remembering our first bikes and who it was that stole them from us, or busted them up just because. The light slipped away suddenly as the dark clouds of the west put a barrier before the sun. The wind picked up, and gritty dust brushed against our bare, scraped knees.

We entered Paul's house, a first-floor rental that stank of decay, cigarette smoke, and fried food. The TV was on just as we had left it, Paul's mother watching and drinking coffee and smoking. There she was, still on the couch, in the now darkened living room, except for the flickering blue of the TV. Yes, there she was, slouched over, facedown, sort of rolled over on her side. Her feet were still on the floor, but her right foot was slightly elevated, resting on its toes. Her pant leg had lifted slightly and I could see one pudgy calf atop her white sock.

Paul, not comprehending, said hello to her. A cigarette burned down slowly from between two yellow stained fingers, one with a ring of silver, and Paul said, "Mom?"

She jerked up for a moment, looking me in the eye, her face dazed through thick glasses, before slouching down again. Paul was rooted to the spot, a chubby kid with freckles and short hair, the top of his head crowned by a baseball cap which he always kept pushed back, his hands closing into fists and opening again. I turned on the light and she jerked up again, once more looking into my eyes, dazed, questioning, and then slouched back into her comfortable, near-fetal position. Perhaps she was being reborn into something new and marvellous as all poor sinners would hope and pray, I suppose, when there's little else to hope for, and Paul shrieked out again, "Mom?!"

Spittle slid out the side of her mouth, and I instinctively went to her and touched her fattened shoulder. I shuddered, because it felt like this touch, with my grasping fingers sinking into her soft flesh, was too intimate, something from which a kid should be protected. Again, she jerked up and looked at me silently, muted, before falling over.

"Call nine-one-one," I told Paul, and suddenly he was a boy of action, heroic, bounding to the phone in a race against time.

The ambulance was on its way, Paul standing by the doorway to the kitchen, a table covered with stacks of dirty supper dishes behind him. He couldn't come to his mother, so I remained seated beside her, my hand on her shoulder. I removed the burning cigarette from between her fingers and observed the coffee table that held a coffee cup, an ashtray, a pack of smokes, a crossword puzzle book, and a plastic bag full of wool and knitting needles. I picked out every detail of that table, not wanting to look at Paul or his mother. I picked up the remote and shut off some investigative show that was analyzing the behaviour of two crazy parents who had tortured their kids.

I looked up and saw a crucifix on the wall with a dried palm leaf haphazardly stuck behind it. I wanted to mumble a prayer into the lady's ear, but I knew none, and then there were sirens and the ambulance arrived.

The paramedics entered almost casually, with expert confidence. They brought form to the scene, moving the coffee table out of the way, crates of equipment in their hands. They felt for a pulse as it began raining a hard rain. They exchanged a glance and a word, and one of them got the stretcher, and they were able to wrestle the two-hundred-pound lady onto it and put her in the ambulance, using a blanket to shelter her from the rain. Paul just stood there, unmoving, and a police car arrived. The officer, in a gentle but forced easy-going voice, asked Paul where his family was. There was no family. A family line that had started a thousand years ago along the banks of the Danube in Croatia had ended right there in Schumacher. The cops would drive Paul to an uncle and aunt's place in Timmins, relatives from his father's side whom he had never met before.

I looked out at the rainy street, mist rising amidst darts of water, and to Paul, who averted his eyes from mine. The officer wanted to help him pack a bag. The ambulance was now gone, its siren heard through the drumming of the rain. Thunder peeled in the distance and then made a sharp crack overhead and the street lit up in a flash of green and blue. The light revealed blank, blackened windows from a rental building across the street—a true dive to be sure, with washers and dryers rusting in the yard, dead hulks emerging from the long, weedy grass. An old woman in a housecoat, standing motionless beneath a red umbrella, watched the proceedings with a sombre look on her face. I told Paul I would go home. In an adult fashion, which seemed to bring a sense of closure for me, I told him to call me if he needed anything.

Paul's mother was pronounced dead at the hospital that night, and my friend moved to Thunder Bay where his father had a labouring job in a mill.

I walked home slowly in the rain. The power was out in Schumacher, so the streets were dark and screaming emptiness. I felt hidden eyes and the whisperings of secrets in all the vacant shop fronts, the boarded-up church and empty apartment windows. I walked down the street past a quiet hotel bar where candles burned like prayers in the window, and in the dim light from up the street, saw two boys running away from me with splashing feet, hockey sticks swinging jubilantly, stick handling an empty pop can. Their legs were dancing, one stick held up to celebrate an imaginary goal before swooping down for a fine slap shot, the can tinkling, skittering, and bouncing as the other boy charged it hungrily. They disappeared in the mist and darkness, and I wonder where they are today.

All ends in death and is at the mercy of death. I observed the ghost of the McIntyre headframe sitting across the lake, a vast bulk, immense in size. It was like a shrine reaching to the heavens, a testament to the great dreams and furious activity of another time that had claimed its own lives. Men had sweated in the darkness belowground. Their families on surface depended on the strong grip of the man down below who daydreamed of sunny Sunday afternoons in Croatia or Italy, while poking the ceiling for loose rock. The men and their wives are no more.

That night when I arrived home, drenched and cold, I pulled out the family Bible from the linen closet and read it for the first time in my life. There was nothing intelligible for my hungry and restless eyes to fasten onto that made any sense to me until, on one of the dividers made of firmer paper, I came across the Hail Mary. I committed the prayer to memory that same night so I would have something to say the next time I accompany someone into death. The prayer has a nice feel to it, and it isn't romantic, or missing the main point.

I didn't go to the funeral because I had lost touch with the whole thing, which is what happens when you're a boy. It was another friend who filled me in on Paul's fate. It's a damned thing, really, losing your mother and then getting shipped off to a father who doesn't want you, or know what to do with you.

Drug Addict

The world is beautiful.

I know I'm from the world, dust to dust, ashes to ashes, but I feel like a visitor to this world every morning when I smell the air, see the clouds, and hear the birds. What a strange experience, to stand in the world and not feel part of it. Like an angel. Grace.

God ... I'm sorry, we fell off the wagon. You know, we were doing good, but we fell off the wagon. Me and Chris, we're going to be married in October next year—not this October. We fell off the wagon a couple of weeks ago.

I wake up on the cot. It is early. Chris is sleeping near me. One of the staff members, the nice one with a kid of her own, is making coffee. I can smell the coffee when she opens the package and dumps it into the filter. Everyone is sleeping, except for the man in the corner, the old, bald one with the long beard. He always has a walking stick. He's scared of practically everyone. Never says a word. He doesn't get in trouble. The cops always leave him alone. He's clean, too. Just a mute, is all, who's scared of people. He sits on his cot and stares off into a space between us. There is rest in the spaces between. He is a saint, I think.

Chris was restless this morning. He woke up and just wanted to go, go, go. Get the day started. The drugs are getting to him. He needs it as soon as he wakes. He's turning. A slow creep up the arms, you know? Up the veins, up the nerves. The nerve endings are jumping, and the slow creep up has got hold of Chris. Aimed right for the brain. And then you flip. You become a fish, belly-up. Dead to the world. He is such a babe. A beautiful, black-haired babe. He always needs someone to care for him. That is what I do. I watch out for him. He needs a woman around. He doesn't get along with men, and can't listen to a man talking for too long. He listens to me, and is safe.

We went to the old railbed. The traffic rushed nearby, disappearing under the bridge. The sun was out and the birds were singing. The green leaves caught the light of the sun. What a colour of green that is! You can't describe it, and you can't mimic it with any man-made colour. I saw the veins in the leaves. I saw a bee buzz by, and a ladybug crawled on a blade of grass. I saw the veins in the leaves and I thought, life is a miracle. And then the wind picked up and the leaves fluttered, and I lost sight of the life of leaves, and life on the earth, and I closed my eyes for a moment and let the wind pass over me. The wind is a spirit.

We sat around in the sun till ten. Tom came by with his wagon. He's returning beer cans he collected at some of his stops. People are kind. They look out for him and leave their beer cans in garbage bags by the front door so Tom can pick them up. He smiled and said hello. Chris just looked at him. Chris was being jealous. Tom said hello and then went to return the beer cans. Then he'll get his fix and he's good to go. Tom is friendly when he's straight. But after he's injected, he gets all hostile, and it's best to stay away from him. At ten we went to George's apartment.

George's hands are shaking. He is a gentle old soul. He offers us a cup of coffee and a cinnamon bun. I'm hungry. The cinnamon tastes so good. It reminds me of my grandmother's baking, out in Vancouver. She is a poor old woman I suppose, but they told her the rundown house she lives in is worth, like, a million dollars now, so then everyone in the family was petrified with fear about what she'd do with the house and they started fighting every day, in the house, in front of grandma! So I got out of there. I travelled to Calgary to find my dad, and that's where I met Chris. Then, me and Chris went off to Winnipeg to see his uncle.

On the prairies, you can see a rainstorm coming from a lifetime away. It feels like you are living in the sky when you are there, on the prairies, with the wind travelling across the land from a thousand miles away. Then we went off to Timmins to find Chris's old friend who worked in the mines. Why should we care what grandma does with her house? She lives in it, and she has for fifty years. She and grandpa, who was in Korea with the army before becoming a janitor at the hospital. He died only five years ago. It is her life, even if she is, like, ninety.

George's coffee tastes good, and the sun comes in through the window of the apartment. I see particles of dust drifting slowly through the air, and then they disappear as they leave the sunbeam. What little worlds exist around us? What can't we see? All the movement makes life beautiful.

George starts to shake more, the longer we wait around. He's very nervous, the sweet old man. Finally, I ask to go to the bathroom, and I clean up with a shower. I come out wearing a towel, and George's face sags with sad eyes that sparkle so he looks like a clown who is feeling mischievous and guilty, scared of being caught. He is such an innocent. I adore George. I wait for him on the bed while Chris goes to the kitchen table. He hasn't eaten anything because he's only worried about the money, and the drugs, of course. George is so innocent, Chris could never be jealous of him.

On top of me George is gentle and terrified. It takes only a few moments, and we are done. George goes to the bathroom. The apartment is quiet. I am happy that I can help George. Lots of men who pay for me are gentle, truth be told. They seem to know how crossed up everything is. But there are also some who are quite mean about it. It's a mask, their mean-ness. They wear masks. I don't wear a mask. I am who I am. The moment you lay your eyes on me you know exactly who I am. But who are you?

I watch people carefully, and I have trouble knowing most people. They wear very good masks. Men are easier to figure out than women. Men are all nervous about something, always moving from one place to the next and scheming. They fight for the daily bread, and then they scheme to get their pleasures. Some of the men are like a bull in a china shop, and take pleasure in hurting others. What are they hiding? Some women are like that too, of course. But there are some gentlemen out there, yes indeed. They are what I imagine old-fashioned men were like more often than not. They are careful to mask their judg-ment, and they nod hello to me to be polite. Some of them care about my well-being and aren't interested in sex or see me as ugly because I have sores on my face and cigarette burns on my arms.

We left George's around 11:30 that morning. He normally pays me forty dollars, but today he gave us forty-seven dollars and fifty cents. "You are a good person," he said to me softly, and he carefully handed the money over. Some men throw the money at me. They want to remind me who I am, in case I start thinking we are equals. Meanwhile, Chris was leaning up against the doorframe, sliding up and down. I could tell he was feeling the creeps pretty bad. He wanted the drugs. He needed them. Oh God, I am so sorry. We fell off the wagon.

The streets were filled with sun. The sun lit up the flowers on the boulevards, and the shop windows sparkled like diamonds as the sun and the wind and the birds and the clouds and even the puppy dogs with their masters all went dancing along. I was a dancer in BC. I could dance every dance. I liked ballet. I liked to hover and turn across the floor with that swaying, gentle music flowing along behind me. I danced till I was twelve. Then my dad left and we couldn't afford dance lessons anymore.

My dad always meant well. He was gentle, but weak. My mom was always yelling at him, and I think a time sometimes comes when a soul breaks, and then it drifts away like a leaf in a stream. Have you seen a leaf in a stream? It is beautiful. But a leaf in a stream is a dance of death. Everything changes, and everything moves, and everything dies. And then it becomes something else. All the movement in nature. I tried to keep track of it once, as a girl. I had my journal and I sat outside and began writing down everything I saw, especially if something was moving. Well, my hand ached, and I couldn't keep up! There were cars and people moving about, of course, and clouds, and leaves on the trees. But then a small cloud of dust, only a hint of yellow dust, picked up and moved in a gentle breeze over the sidewalk, and a bird sang and flew through the air, and a butterfly fluttered this way and that over the nodding flowers, and then I lowered my face to the warm, damp-feeling grass and wow! There was more life in that green jungle than I could even begin to describe. And what about the worms under the grass? And the bugs who live in the dark, shadowy places? You see what I mean. I just wrote and wrote, and I couldn't keep up! Life is so beyond me. I can only try to keep up.

We crossed Third Avenue and a guy across the street yelled at me. Skanky whore! He laughed. Chris looked at him and muttered under his breath, and he kept bouncing along, up and down with deep dips. I think he has to go the bathroom. Why didn't he go at George's? Honestly, I have to always watch Chris. He is always forgetting things. I was going to yell something back to the guy, but the truth of it was that I was feeling the creeps now, too. Chris bounces when he gets the creeps. Me, I start walking fast and in straight lines, urging Chris along.

The guy yelled again, not words, just a growl to the sky for God to hear. I have seen him at the shelter recently, and he drinks mouthwash every day. He'll rot his brains out drinking that poison. We went up the street till we got to the back house on First. It is in an alleyway behind an old pool hall. It looks all poor and ramshackle, and I suppose it is, but there's a dealer living there now, though he'll be moving soon enough. They're always moving, but always easy to find. Chris went to go to the bathroom behind a dumpster and I knocked on the door. A guy answered right away, since this is peak business time. I gave him twenty. He says, how 'bout a blow instead? I can't tell if he's teasing me or not, so I just ask for the drugs. I will not be strung along for someone's amusement. Within two seconds the fix is in my hand and he's closing the door, saying goodbye, so I don't know if that was a real offer or if he was just being mean. What an asshole.

Chris was all over me. Did you get it? Did you get it? he asked, like, ten times. This got me jumping too, of course. Anyway, I gave him the drugs, and we walked quickly back across town to the railbed. Ideally, we'd go to someone's apartment or camp, but we left the shelter so early this morning, and were running around everywhere we went it seems, that we'd met no one familiar. So, we went to a well-used place, behind the church. We found a quiet place underneath some thick trees and sat down on some rocks. Chris got the needle ready. I can't do that, and I can't inject, but luckily there is always someone around who can. I was really jumping now. Let's get this show on the road, yessiree! The train is coming!

Chris is a gentleman. He injects me first, because he knows once he's gotten it he's of no help to me.

The surge comes right up into my head, behind my eyes like a rainbow volcano, a burst of purple lava, and yellow, and green, and red. Oh, that is it. There it is. I flow. I am flowing now, like the wind that sails unseen over the town, making little waves on the water and fluttering the leaves, and the birds soar on my outstretched hands as I reach for the heavens. I watch Chris inject, too, and he rolls off the stone he's sitting on and leans against it from the ground. He nods his head. Yeah, yeah, yeah, I think he's saying. This is all good. It is all good now. I lie down beside him, in his arms.

Sometime later, I don't know how long, suddenly we're being jostled awake. It's the cops. They're clearing out the trees of users, I guess so the walkway will remain respectable for families walking by from downtown to the lake. I get it, I really do. But the cops are so insulting, talking to me like I'm a child. You can't be shooting up here, says a cop with disgust in his voice. That's what bothers me, the disgust in his voice. They push us. Move! Move! Move! I have a plastic bag, and I'm thinking of the families who walk by here. They shouldn't see the garbage here. That would be bad, so I start picking up litter.

I lie to the cops. I'm not a drug user! I say. Leave me alone! Leave me alone! And the cop laughs. Good one, he says. I go and pick up litter on the pathway, which is not where the cops want me going. They want me up and out of the place. I pick up litter. Donut bags, coffee cups, mouthwash bottles, needles, chip bags, pop cans. Soon my bag is full. Get out of here now! roars a cop. I am the only one left. Everyone else has gone. You don't have to be mean about it, I say, and then I go up the hill to the street. Where is Chris? I don't know. Being alone terrifies me, but right away I am at ease, because I see a yard sale just a few houses away.

It is hot, but a gentle breeze blows. The wind is a spirit. There are scarves and clothes hanging from lines all around the yard, sailing gently on the breeze. It feels like I'm entering a gypsy camp. Pigeons rest on the roof of the house and look down on the milling people amid the colours. There are books on tables, candles, and children's toys. I had two children. My first was when I was fourteen, my second when I was sixteen. Life is so beautiful that I can't let it go. I knew that when I was fourteen, and had already spent half a year on the street. Because of that, I made sure I never looked upon my baby's face, or I knew I'd never let it go. But it was best for the baby to go to a family. I knew that.

There is a book at the yard sale about God, about God re-creating the world at every moment, and I like that because that's what I feel when I look at this world of ours. Everything is brand new, always, so I pick up the book and I feel better. A nice lady says hello to me and says I should try some of the dresses. You are so pretty! she says. These dresses won't fit me, she says, but they'll fit you. You have a beautiful figure! I am in a gypsy camp and I see this lady, and she has no masks. I see her and know her, and I know she can see me, too, but only knows love, and I wonder at the magic of it all, how angels appear every day, unexpected. What did we do to deserve such an honour? I thank God for everything, and I am sorry that I sometimes forget about God, but this feeling of being sorry is a sweet feeling, like a blues love song, because I know that it is sadness over forgetting God that makes me rush back to God. We are never alone, even when we are.

Chris arrived as though out of thin air. He doesn't say anything, he just sways and bobs as though he's about to collapse on the ground and then seep through the grass into the earth like water, and keep sliding away till he re-emerges in the water that flows through the centre of town, in the river beneath the tall bridge. He leans on me and leans on the banister of the front steps of the house. He is sliding, and mute. I tell the kind woman about our marriage next October, not this October, and I apologize that we fell off the wagon, but we're going to get clean, yes, next week. Chris? What do you think of this white dress? It fits me wonderfully, holding me like a hug.

I was twelve when I got my last hug from my dad, before he left. He was crying. He had nothing, and was hitchhiking back to Calgary. Then I got pregnant and went to the streets, because my mom wanted to kill me. For a while I stayed in touch with my grandma. She was a kind old soul. She knew how dangerous everything was, and she carried a sadness. It wasn't supposed to be this way, she said, holding a teacup with old, veined, and capable hands. She could sew and bake and garden, and somehow, she said, things hadn't turned out for her children. She didn't understand, and neither do I. What happens when things turn for the worse? Is God looking away? No, God is always there. I think people turn away. God watches and cries for people. People turn away from God because they are free. My counsellor told me I am not free because I am an addict. But I disagree. I am also free. I am not free of drugs, true enough, but life is bigger than drugs, and my counsellor forgets that all the time. Whether I'm high or not, I always have choices to make, and I can turn from God, or not turn away. The world is beautiful. I'm sorry, God. Don't cry for us. Let me cry for you, instead.

The lady appears with two glasses of water for us, water with large clinking ice cubes. Chris takes a sip, leaning on the banister, bobbing up and down, his eyes to the ground, and I can see the lady is worried he'll drop the glass, but he doesn't, and the sun shines on his head and he seems beaten down by the heat, and all the colours fluttering in the breeze around him can't lift him up. What do you think of this dress? I ask again. Now I'm wearing a purple dress with nice fringes on the edge. Chris doesn't know what to say. He hems and haws. He wants to go. Chris, I say, you need clothes too! Let's get you some pants. He has been wearing the same clothes for two weeks and never changes them, I say to the lady.

The lady points to where all the men's pants are, hanging on a line off a lilac bush, in front of a wrought iron fence. I drag Chris over to the pants, but he could care less. Come on, Chris, I say, try these on. But he says no, let's go. I see the cops at the end of the street. They are watching the yard sale from their cars, wondering what me and Chris will do next. I don't like it when they call me names, I say to Chris. They don't have to be mean about it. I just wanted to pick up some garbage. We weren't shooting drugs down there, I say to the lady, and the lady just smiles and says, I'm sorry. Thank you, I say. Thank you. She is sorry, and she means it. Chris is walking down the street, toward the police.

Chris has stopped halfway toward the cops. He is leaning on a tree. The cops aren't doing anything. They're visiting with one another, leaning on their cars.

The earth keeps trying to drag Chris down toward her. The earth wants to hug Chris; she wants to have Chris lie on her and feel her turning and spinning through the universe. You are with me and part of me, says the earth to Chris.

I have a bag full of clothes, plus some nice sweatpants for Chris. I am wearing the purple dress over my pants and tank top, and I also have my book about God re-creating the world at every moment. Then the lady gives me a nice necklace with a matching bracelet. There are dark brown stones set in the silver. I feel like I'm being blessed. The lady says the stones come from the Holy Land. I reach into my pocket and find seven dollars and fifty cents. I think Chris has the extra twenty that George gave us. I offer the money to the lady, and she smiles gently, and there might be a tear in her eye, and she says, no, you keep the money. I feel like a queen with this jewellery on.

"I want you to be well," she says.

I'm sorry, I say. We fell off the wagon. We were doing good, but we fell off the wagon, and we're going to get clean again. We will, and we're going to be married next October, of next year.

That is wonderful, says the lady. She is smiling again. It will be exciting to be married, she says, and I agree and thank her again, and I leave to find Chris.

The bag of clothes feels good on my arm. We are set up nicely now. I also have money. The farmer's market isn't far away, with trucks and trailers, and children holding their mother's hands, and baby ducks in a little pool, and lambs in the pens for the children to pet. I pet the lambs, too. I rub their little woolly heads, with pink mouths that suck my fingers. It is just past the bridge. Last week we bought a watermelon at the market. Chris loved that watermelon. We sat beneath a tall green shade tree near the river and ate the whole watermelon, sun glinting off the blue river, red flesh, green skin, spitting black slippery seeds at yellow dandelions that grew nearby. I am going to buy Chris a watermelon and we'll eat it, and then Chris will return to me, at least till the morning, when the smell of ground coffee will welcome me to a new beautiful day.

I catch up to Chris. Where's the fuckin' twenty dollars? he suddenly yells at me.

I'm sorry Chris, you have it. I don't have it.

I can't find it! he yells. Chris is very angry. He raises his fist like he's ready to smack me. It is like he suddenly woke up, but there is only violent rage, like a demon rage, left for him and the world. I don't understand. Why is Chris being mean to me? I feel alone. Everyone saw him raise his fist, too. I am embarrassed.

The police stand up straight, and watch Chris carefully. Where's the money? he yells.

Check your pockets, I say.

He thrusts his hands into his pockets and he finds the twenty. Of course he did. I knew I didn't have it. And then Chris turns and runs as fast as he can, past the cops and onto the old railbed. There is a cloud of dust as he falls down. He had been going too fast, and stumbled on the way down. Why is he running? The police are looking at each other. They aren't sure what to do. I'm sorry, I say to the police. I will find him. They nod okay. I go down to the railbed. The

83

police are no longer down there, and three guys have moved in and are now shooting up in another bush, right beside the walls of the church. If you don't look for them you can't find them, but I can see them. Chris has given them the twenty, and he's taking another hit. I cry. I call him.

Chris! Chris! Please, let's go to the farmer's market! He doesn't even look at me. He has flipped. I didn't think it would happen this fast. Chris slides down to the ground and the other guys laugh. They're stoned, and now they're eyeing me. But I can't give anymore. I'm tired, and want to eat watermelon.

The world is beautiful. I am still crying, but it feels good to cry. Tears are real. Tears don't care about masks, and tears heal. I walk over the railway bridge, and through my tears I see the tall, straight, brown apartment building rising into the pale blue sky with its nicely ordered windows. It is right out of a picture, that's how nice and ordered it is. The sun has begun to move into the western sky, and the cool shadows of buildings and trees begin to lengthen. Where has this day gone? Like all the days, it passed by, steady as a metronome. As the world moves and the days pass, people are jostled about, to and fro, bumping into each other and drifting apart, some rising as spirits and others looking for a way to get through.

What is in a day? Why is a day like a gauntlet that you have to pass through? Why is a day something to endure, or something to lose? Why can't a day embrace us and never let go? There is a difference between what we want and what we need. That's what my counsellor said. I know that. Everyone knows that, and you don't need to be a counsellor to understand that. I hear the men behind me, yelling insults at me and beckoning me back to the bushes. They have twenty dollars for me, they say. But I don't feel like twenty dollars. When I don't turn back, a couple of them throw stones at me. I am a bird, a free bird, and I am going to keep sailing. I will watch each day and live in each day like a bird that flies, and perches on the branches, and is happy because it knows it is cared for. That is how I will live the day.

It was when I got to the shelter that night that I heard. A tough girl who thinks she runs the place blurted out to me about Chris. I acted like I didn't hear, or like I already knew, and I went into the shelter, and there was the nice lady with a child of her own. I looked at her, and she looked at me with sadness, and I knew then that this was it. Chris was far away now, and the worst thing of all is that I couldn't feel him near me. His presence, I mean. I always thought you could feel the dead near you, but I can't feel Chris, and I'm afraid of what that means. The old man with the walking stick is already sitting on his cot. He always settles in early so he will get the cot in the corner. He looks at me and he doesn't say anything, but he's looking at me as if he's saying, hey, look at me and know that everything will be good. You are safe, his eyes say.

Maybe he will watch over me through the night. Maybe he does every night. I need to rest. I need to lie down. I don't want anything anymore. Who am I? I thought I knew.

Benediction

The Christmas Dragon

(Told to me by a woman in the ICU.)

grew up in a northern town, far from the glitter of towering cities. I grew up surrounded by forests that sprawled into the lost horizons of James Bay, and I grew up near lakes and fast-flowing rivers. In the spring, when the snow melted and the lakes opened up, I would be awoken by bears upsetting the garbage cans in my backyard. Every summer I would observe moose calmly chewing their evening meal in the ditches by the road, and hear owls hoot, ravens caw, and in the winter, wolves howl. And at any point in the year, I might be fortunate enough to see a shy lynx slink about.

Many of my adventures were unique to the North. One cold autumn, when the air was filled with the sweet scent of decaying leaves, I was lost for a night while accompanying my father on a partridge hunt. Another time, I was swept down a river when my canoe capsized, boulders deep and silent beneath the rush of water rising up like ominous spirits to bump me to and fro. While helping my mother with the blueberry picking one hot August afternoon, I was cornered by an angry black bear whom I had surprised while it fed its always ravenous hunger. I have camped beneath a night sky far from any sources of man-made light, and have seen starscapes that might astound you. I have followed lonely, shuffling prospectors around town who have never spent more than a couple weeks at a time in civilization before heading back into the bush. But as much as these experiences contributed to the formation of my character and sense of the world, nothing about the North could have prepared me for my last childhood Christmas, and this is what my story is about.

The house I grew up in with my younger brother was a little one. This meant that when we weren't reading or tinkering with some hobby, we were outside. Our neighbourhood was full of children to play with. Amidst the charitable and kindly neighbours, we also had neighbours who seemed quite insane, and lived in houses that were haunted. There were stray cats and dogs, secret passages between yards, and coded methods of communicating as we spied on all who passed on the streets of our town.

Every winter a massive, rounded mound of snow would begin to grow beneath the towering cedars of our yard. This snowdrift resembled the back of a breaching whale. It was built by the wind, helped along with snow my father piled up while keeping the back porch clear. Beginning every December, my brother and I would start to dig tunnels and trenches in this heavily packed snow.

In mid-December of 1978, we began digging a tunnel after the first blizzard of the winter. We worked at a snowdrift six feet high that the north wind had piled for us on the leeward side of our fence. The wind had shaped the snow beautifully. At the apex of the sloping and arched drift was a tapered ridge that made the drift look like some futuristic cathedral. We sprayed water over the roof of our holy sanctuary, anointing it while at the same time protecting it from any physical harm. In the minus twenty-degree air, the sprayed water hardened the roof of our pleasure dome like a turtle's shell.

As the snow continued to fall throughout the following week, my brother and I continued to dig. We created a tunnel that led to a cavern beneath the snow cathedral's vaulted ceiling that was the longest and roomiest we had ever made. At the day's end, when the moon began to rise and the muted glow of Christmas lights surrounded us with a mystical embrace, we would head inside. We felt deeply satisfied with our work, and excited by the mystery of our creation that lay hidden from the eyes of the world. Our mother would make us each a cup of hot chocolate, even though family supper was less than an hour away, and we would share smiles with each other, knowing what privileges and gifts awaited us at this time of year. Christmas was coming, and our new snow cavern was part of the magic of that season. It was something we knew would be woven into the warm memories of Christmases past. We were so excited that school seemed like only a minor inconvenience for the feasting and celebrating that would be coming to our home as sure as the sun rises every morning.

Less than a week before Christmas, my brother and I ran home from school for a bite to eat so we could return quickly to our digging of the snow cave. The days were short at this time of the year, so every minute counted. Only the day before, our cave had reached the foot of the fence and we were anxious to continue the tunnel into our neighbour's yard. This crossing of the property line would be done by digging through a hole in the fence beside the neighbour's shed. During summer games of tag or hide-and-seek, this hole served as an excellent secret passageway.

Following our quick snack, we headed off into the backyard, slipped quietly into the cathedral entrance, and crawled deep into the tunnel. We carried our shovels like a pair of dwarves intent on searching for gold. We came into the main cavern and rested a moment, turning on flashlights, even though a luminous green light from the world above still showed itself through the thin patches in the ceiling. We had already started various passageways off the main cavern, and began working on the one that would lead us in the direction of the hole in the fence.

We took turns digging with the spade while the other gathered the loose snow near the tunnel entrance with empty ice cream buckets. Feeling safe under the snow from the ears of the world, we excitedly planned and wondered aloud the directions of our various passageways. We speculated on the truth of the weather forecast that called for more snow, and pondered who of our friends should be allowed entrance into this playground made of ice and snow. Our snow cavern excited us so much that we had not even dared tell our friends for fear of someone wrecking it, accidentally or otherwise.

As the light outside dimmed, our labours intensified, and we grew quiet and determined. Then, at last, we reached the wall of our neighbour's shed. We had dug a six-foot tunnel off the main cavern, and despite breaking through the snow a couple of times, we remained essentially hidden from the world.

Suppertime was soon to come. We prepared to cease in our labours when the door of the shed beside us opened, its rusty hinges moaning like evil spirits. My brother, who was leading the tunnelling, turned quickly and looked at me with a mock-horrified expression on his face. His smiling face was aglow in the beam of my flashlight. From his excited eyes, I could tell that he saw nothing but amusing possibilities in the current situation. I, on the other hand, being blessed with a rather reserved nature, was anxious to avoid any embarrassments with the neighbour. I quickly put my finger to my lips and shook my head vigorously. My brother, like all boys his age, was deeply inspired by the noble deeds of men in perilous situations. I do not doubt that in the face of my warning he was at least momentarily stirred by the possibility that this was just such a dangerous circumstance. His smile ceased in an instant and a heroic-like setting of the jaw emerged instead. He nodded understanding like a soldier receiving orders under fire, and I turned off the flashlight silently.

Coming from the shed beside us, we could hear and feel heavy, hollow footsteps through the snow walls of our passageway.

"This is crazy!" muttered my neighbour forcibly, as though he had been holding his breath for too long. He and his wife were young, and normally cool and aloof. The panic in his voice was a novel thing for me to hear.

"Shut your trap and relax!" a stranger replied anxiously, with a low, forced-hush voice.

"I like my job! I like my life! This is nuts!" my neighbour quickly chattered back like an anxious squirrel, his voice shrill and uncontrolled.

"If you don't get a hold of yourself, you'll lose it all! Now shut up and listen! We made it out—we're safe. We just have to hide this and—"

"For how long though?" my neighbour interrupted, giggling unnaturally, almost hysterically.

"It doesn't really matter—no one knows we have it anyway. Calm down!" The stranger was growing agitated, a fearful and desperate tone in his voice.

They were silent for a moment. I heard something being lifted and dropped back down with a heavy thud. Then my neighbor spoke up again, this time his words ringing with relief.

"They said the mine was going too deep. Now I believe them. It was too weird down there. When has a pile of gold like that ever been found? Just lying there as if someone stacked it up on purpose?"

"Don't forget, no one has seen it yet. Those are our workings down there. There won't be no other crew going on into that crevice."

"That was brilliant, blocking that stope with a danger sign. That's all ours, now." My neighbour was growing excited again, the shrillness of his voice a rising crescendo as though the speed of his thoughts could not keep up with the waggling of his tongue.

"Shut up! Slow down! You're making me nervous. We'll just keep biding our time—we'll get it out. We have at least six months to do it, and with us having a company truck, it'll be easy to smuggle out."

"Where can we hide it though? This is crazy!"

There was silence for a moment, and some shuffling of feet.

"Keeping it in this shed is probably not a good idea," the stranger admitted. "Crooks and nosey kids are always going into places like this."

I could hear them exit the shed. Suddenly, I heard a footstep in the snow, right where my brother was lying. An explosive rush of noise ahead and a cold draught of air washed over my face. It felt as though my ears had just popped on an ascending airplane.

"Simple! We'll leave it here under the snow for now. Next week we'll take it to my uncle's hunting camp, after the roads are ploughed."

Without another word, they walked away. It was impossible to hear anything more in the tunnel, until we heard the back door of the house shut fast.

I turned on the flashlight and gasped when I saw that a canvas bag was sitting right in front of my brother, within our grasp. It had been shoved into the snow immediately over our tunnel.

For a moment, we looked at the bag, and then my brother looked at me. I was dumbfounded and gave no expression or remark. My brother reached for the bag.

"Leave it!" I whispered urgently. His hand hesitated and then withdrew. We backed out of the tunnel, met in the cavern, and headed inside for supper. We didn't speak of the sack or our tunnel for the remainder of the evening, until we had been tucked into bed. After our parents returned downstairs, I snuck into my brother's room.

"What should we do?" he asked me.

"I don't know. If we tell someone we might get in trouble with the neighbour. You heard how scared he is." I looked to my brother for affirmation.

Gold fever had temporarily rendered him deaf and blind to any of my warnings. "I think we should take it for ourselves!" he replied.

This was not what I was hoping to hear. "That's bad! That's dangerous! We could get in big trouble!"

"No one will know!" my brother said, grabbing my arm. "He won't tell the police, and we'll just act like we don't know anything!"

"Except our tunnel is there, and he'll put the pieces together himself, duh!"

My brother fell silent, but as he bit his lower lip in studious concentration and tapped his fingers together, I could tell he was scheming.

"We'll do nothing at all for now. We won't even go into the tunnel for a week, till the gold is out of there!" I urged, grabbing his arm in the hope that he would heed my words.

My brother looked at me, but his eyes were drifting far away, lost in dreams of personal fortune. I wasn't sure he had heard anything I said. My stomach tightened with nervousness.

"We don't even know it is gold," he pondered. "It might just be a real tasty sandwich." We burst out laughing over that joke, trying to muffle our giggles in the blanket so Mom and Dad wouldn't hear. We knew it was gold, but the tension had momentarily been lifted.

The nervousness I felt over my brother's intentions was confirmed the next day after school when he declared he was going back into the snow tunnels. I pleaded with him to reconsider, but he was adamant. And when I threatened him, as a big sister will do on occasion, he only grew more determined. Finally, I was able to convince him to wait until after supper, when the sun had long set and we could sneak in without fear of anyone seeing us in the yard.

We finished our homework and piano practices before supper, hurriedly helped Mom clean and put away dishes, and then bundled up for outside.

The moon was rising in the east, full and bright. In the dark green and purpling sky around the moon's light, wisps of cloud glowed like distant landscapes on a lost horizon. Far in the eternal night, stars wavered in the frigid air like fireflies frozen in time. The branches popped and squeaked in the cedar tree behind us as a rising breeze from the north began to move grains of snow drifting about the tunnel entrance. The blown snow shifted in starts with a rasping sound over our frozen-solid cathedral roof.

My brother had dropped down into our sacred grotto, scurrying through the entrance like a squirrel to its nest. Almost overwhelmed by the beauty of the night around me, I could not help but take one last, longing look at the full moon. But as my eyes began to turn excitedly toward the snow, a dark shadow in the night sky caught my attention. At first, I thought an owl must have passed overhead, but as my eyes adjusted, I could see that the shadow was actually far away, drifting lazily in wide arcs far above the earth in the moon's glow. I was stunned. I could not fathom what I was seeing, but as the shadow moved slowly and assuredly through the light of the moon, I could make out unmistakably the long tail and wide sweeping wings of a dragon.

I want to make it clear that, as a growing girl, I rarely indulged fantasies of fear or delight. I did not while away my days lost in childish reveries, nor was I a quickly panicked child who would jump at the slightest provocation. I was in grade seven, and though I had great patience and empathy for the romantic experiences of artists and poets, I was, in the end, guided by common sense in the here and now of the material universe. I have no need of visions nor fantastic tales. All I can say to you the reader is that I saw the silent but swift shadow of a dragon before the moon and accepted my observations as fact, however incredible.

This ability to accept what was, in essence, unacceptable, saved my life. Although the observed dragon was nearly a mile away at first sighting, after what was maybe three of my own shallow breaths in time long, the dragon was quickly a bulk of presence so physically large the houses and trees around me seemed to cower in submission before it. I just managed to duck into the snow cathedral when, from the dragon's open mouth, the fires of hell reigned down upon my neighbour's house in a fiery blast of great concentration. In an instant, the house was an inferno, our family's home a soon-to-burst tinderbox.

The heat of the fire stung my cheeks in the tunnel entrance, so I turned and crawled deeper into our snow cathedral. I emerged in the open cavern to find my brother staring awestruck at the ceiling, which was now glowing bright orange. We had no need of our flashlights. Inside this ice womb we felt safe and comfortable in the midst of the destruction outside. We stole a glance at one another. Both of us were uncomprehending and in shock, yet we had an innocent desire to laugh, too. Our smiles of disbelief were tinged with a questioning awe. We had escaped something horrible. The experience of liberation made us feel giddy.

A concussion like a dull thud shook the frozen earth, and alerted us to the fact that something large and heavy was nearby. A shivering shadow, dark and awesome, fell over our beautiful, orange cathedral ceiling. In fear, my brother and I scurried into a side tunnel, the one that led to the hole in the fence. Feeling protected beside the shed, we slowed, and with bated breath strained to hear evidence of further movement outside. We could only hear the crackle of wood burning when a voice called out for a moment, like a lost sailor's cry in a stormy gale. The fire burned so hot that condensation began to form in our little tunnel. But then a new sound could be heard—a sniffing sound, close and intimate, such as when a dog sniffs your ear. Yet this sniffing was deeper, like a horse's breathing as it considers the hay offered to it in a child's upturned hand.

Just as I was about to whisper that there was a dragon outside our sanctuary—a fact that seemed more fantastic the longer I stayed in that tunnel—there was a heavy jolt right over top of us. The end of our tunnel disappeared, and was replaced by a scaly claw the size and power of which could easily have grabbed us both and crushed us to death.

As daintily as a crawling baby will pick a cookie crumb from a carpet, so this large evil instrument picked up the little canvas bag from the snow, withdrawing it silently and swiftly. We looked up and saw the claw rise to the angular and shrewd face of a scaled dragon, a dragon that was steaming and salivating thoughtfully as it sniffed the sack lightly.

His cunning and lively eyes focused intently on his reclaimed gold with a ring of self-satisfied humour about them, an egotistical humour that comes with a great, all-knowing confidence. With the flames behind him reaching up into the night with furious passion, the dragon seemed to breathe deeply with a sense of peace, aglow in an unholy nimbus of his own making.

Satisfied with its possession, the dragon looked down to the raging fire, his long, spiked tail swaying gracefully in the air behind him, seeming to reflect his contemplative state. In a hollow and guttural voice, the dragon muttered a curse on the destroyed house in a language I could scarcely understand. The language resembled an old English, and as I listened to the dragon and remembered his words, the more understandable they grew. The curse went something like this: "You have caused me to awake! And you have taken my trove! Uncouth race of man! By greed and lust, you fall!"

My brother and I embraced instinctively, for we were suddenly struck by new fear that this violence was personal. The dragon wanted revenge for the disturbance of his treasure. We feared that he would see us as the culprits responsible. Alas, as events quickly unfolded, it was clear the dragon understood the matter well. With a swiftness that defied the immense girth of this primordial beast, he thrust his head and a claw into the flames of the burning house, and after a moment of fishing about, withdrew his arm, clutching the bodies of my neighbours.

With a blast so powerful that the breath was stolen from me, the wings beat down with one ferocious flail, rippling like the sails of an old masted ship, and the dragon bounded away into the night sky. The light of the fire, the pitch-black smoke, the smoldering of the homes in our neighbourhood, and the blinking of the just-arrived fire truck all served to distract witnesses from the awesome sight above their heads. But I scampered up through the snow beside the glistening roof of our icy grotto to see a swaying and drifting dragon in flight, quickly gaining altitude and accelerating north into the same icy gales now fanning the flames onto our home.

In the days that followed, my brother and I mostly kept the story to ourselves. We warily mentioned the dragon to our parents and a couple of close friends, curious how the story of such a beast would be taken. As expected, there was not the slightest shred of patience on the part of others for believing such a tale. We became quiet. My brother and I could only share knowing glances with one another over the supper table at my grandmother's house—our family's temporary residence—when it was mentioned that the fire chief had stated the cause of fire to be a furnace oil explosion. Further to the point, it was deemed to be a fire set purposely by the young couple next door. This was because no bodies were found, and the young couple could not be accounted for anywhere. Stories began to spread through town that they had run away from tremendous debt.

By Christmas Eve, the shock over our experience began to wane. Christmas was saved by the good humour and love of our parents, and the baking my grandmother fervently attended to. Lightly browned pastries dripped with butter icing, blueberry pies were made with the summer's harvest, and of course a turkey roasted in the oven. Our gaze was drawn to the humble yet beautifully trimmed Christmas tree nestled in the small living room between the piano and the stereo, where Bing Crosby crooned about Christmas in Killarney.

Our family bundled up for Christmas Eve mass, where my brother and I served at the altar. The church glowed warmly with an inner light, candles gleaming through the hushed air around the Nativity scene. Rosy-cheeked parishioners sang Joy to the World, Silent Night, and Away in a Manger. We exchanged happy Christmas wishes with our friends, and urged our parents along after mass, when it seemed all they wanted to do was stay and visit with people. All was well, a testament to the love born in this season of grace and mystery. For this one time of year our northern town, as it was every year, seemed to be a village of one mind and heart.

Following mass, our family returned home and adjourned to my grandmother's dining room where the adults drank coffee and visited happily. My brother and I were restless. For reasons I could not appreciate at the time as well as I can now, we seemed to read each other's mind with a clarity only matched by language itself. Hardly needing to ask permission on such a night as Christmas Eve, we bundled up in our winter clothes and headed out into the quiet, expectant streets of our village.

Was it nostalgia that drew us back to our snow cathedral? Curiosity? Or was it a desire for healing after the trauma of the fire and subsequent devouring of our neighbours by a reptilian beast that knew no mercy nor appreciation for the dignity bestowed on man? As I reflect now, I am beginning to appreciate that the powers of the dragon may have extended beyond the merely physical. Was there something subtle and immeasurable that beckoned those still involved in the thieving of the dragon's trove to return to the scene of the worm's destructive rage?

We entered our yard and passed the burned-out hulk of our former home, my brother in the lead. The smell of ash and smoke filled the air, and the snow, despite another brief snowfall, was darkened by soot. This part of our neighbourhood was abandoned temporarily, as the fire and smoke damage had affected homes up and down the street.

It was very quiet.

Slowly approaching the snow cathedral, we inspected its roof. The heat of the fire had only served to harden it even more, the melting snow quickly freezing once again so that six inches of solid ice now protected the sanctuary within. A more beautiful snowdrift could not have been found, with the light of the moon glistening off of it like a vigil candle before Saint Francis in the darkened church.

We entered the cavern and rested, commenting on the warmth to be found there. We were tired, and quickly fell silent, not interested in the slightest to explore the tunnels branching off from our main room. Mysteriously, sleep seemed to wash over us, a paralyzing sleep that made us aware of our surroundings yet, as if in a dream, rendered us incapable of action. So it was that the second thief found us at his mercy.

The footsteps and heavy breathing of the second gold thief were not noticed by us until he had dropped down to his knees to enter our cathedral. We were alarmed, and began to awaken slowly from our dream-like slumber. We could smell him. Tobacco and the sweet scent of whiskey announced his arrival as much as his panting breath and laboured crawling in the confines of the tunnel built for children, not a two-hundred-pound man. Our holy place beneath the icy snow was desecrated at that moment. His presence had a grossly sacrilegious quality that cut like a knife through the mystery and beauty of life, leaving only the wearisome business of getting to the bottom of who now had the treasure, and where it was cached.

To save the burglar the trouble, I calmly said, "We don't have the gold."

The thief exhaled slowly and with relief, as if he too wanted to avoid the tedious nature of our conflict. "So where is it then, squirt?" His voice sounded tired.

My brother, bouncing the flashlight about on his knee, broke the calm and measured pace of our conversation with the exclamation, "A dragon came and took it!"

I shut my eyes. I knew what the thief was going to say before he said it. My brother, sobering up after giving voice to what was impossible to understand, also understood.

"I don't care about playing no games with stupid children. I know where to get more gold. But I ain't gonna let no little squirts skip around town talking about no high-grade gold neither—guaranteed!" Magically, he now had a hunting knife in his hand.

Out of fear, I suppose, I giggled. An image of Tom Sawyer and Becky running from revengeful Joe in the caves made me wonder where reality began and where it ever ended. It was here, though, that the dragon magic in the air began to weave its spell on the thief. It is not that he fell asleep or became hypnotized, but he grew thoughtful in a deeply meditative way. Intoxicated by either dragon magic or dragon poison, I could read his thoughts. He had become aware of the paltry and limited nature of his greed, and the meaningless violence it birthed.

And he became aware of the power that my brother and I possessed in that holy place under the ice. Not a power to physically defeat him, of course, but a timeless power that was invincible because it was goodness, innocence, and hopefulness. It was a power the burglar had probably once possessed himself, and it was certainly a power he yearned for in the quiet of his heart. It was the mystery of good and evil ringing his dulled thoughts as it did for the first primordial caveman who suddenly awoke with the disquieting sense of self-consciousness born from violence against his own kind.

His eyes flitted up to us and he exhaled deeply, the fumes of tobacco and whiskey ever present. He was aware of the distastefulness of his presence in this sanctuary, but as a weathervane will turn on a gust of wind, so too his manner quickly grew more determined than ever. He was willing himself to action, despite the fact that he now seemed to know the futile nature of following evil into the shadows of self-destruction. He gripped the knife with a firm hold and made to grab me.

It was then that the earth groaned, and we sensed over top of us the familiar bulk of presence that was the dragon. There was no "thud" as he landed, however, and I realized that the dragon had been resting and watching us from the backyard of our former neighbour's house. It was the poisonous vapours exuding from his thick, scaled skin that had inspired such drowsy reveries for all three of us present. My brother and I looked with gaping mouths and wide eyes to the ceiling. The thief looked up as best he could in the now-cramped space of the sanctuary. For an immensely quiet moment it felt like we were aboard a stricken ocean steamer in the hesitating instant before it turned and plunged underneath the icy dark waters.

Then the sniffing of the dragon could be heard through the ceiling. He was seeking out the meaning of our cathedral. After another brief pause, a sharp scraping sound began overhead, like skates cutting into the ice of a frozen lake, meandering along the length of the glazed roof.

"Who dwells in this hermitage?" the dragon bellowed, the force of his thundering voice threatening to cave in our snow grotto.

We couldn't crawl out because the burglar was in our way, so I looked up and yelled through the ice, "Me and my brother!" I did this for self-preservation only, not inspired by bravery or impudence. I hoped that this intelligent beast would hesitate to smash in our hallowed chamber if the occupants of it cooperated with him to the best of their ability.

"I smell the two of you, indeed. But there is a third!" the dragon growled.

I turned my gaze from the ceiling to the thief, who looked at me with a questioning and fearful look.

My brother shone the light directly into the thief's face, causing him to squint stupidly. "It's the dragon," my brother said to him, a patient, hopeful tone in his voice. We really did want the intruder to understand.

The thief of the dragon's trove looked to me under the shade of his hand with a question that, again, I could comprehend even though no words had been voiced.

"Hiding in here won't make him go away," I said.

"I think he does what he wants," my brother added.

We looked at the thief, and all three of us came silently to the conclusion that it was better to move out and face the beast.

The thief was out first, but I deliberately did not look at his face as I clambered out of the tunnel. Nor did I look up at the dragon as he moved his incredible bulk closer toward us, causing the earth to tremble. Instead, I crouched at the entrance and helped my brother stand up. Only then did I plant my feet firmly and turn to gaze upon the beast, whose rank odour now filled the air. He smelled like a body unwashed for a thousand years, and when he leaned over us, the sharp, acrid stench was enough to make my eyes water. I even felt pity for him as we do for an old person unable to care properly for themselves. But when my eyes took in the magnificent grandeur

THE BURDEN OF LIGHT

of this ancient lizard, all pity was swept away by a mixture of awe and fear.

He was immense, larger than our former house, and his scales shimmered in the light of the night. His colour oscillated from greens to purples, to shades of gold to reds before dropping to black as he moved ever so slightly, resettling himself into a more comfortable sitting posture. Even this slight movement of the dragon was enough to cause boards and other wreckage from the burned houses and destroyed fence to shift noisily beneath him, but once the dragon had settled, he had the ability to remain motionless and almost imperceptible against the dark background that was our abandoned neighbourhood. I noticed that vapours were rising from his body in thin wisps, disappearing in the cold night air.

"This hermitage would be yours?" he asked with his low, hollow, and gravelly voice, seeming to accuse more than ask me.

"Me and my brother's," I replied sheepishly.

"Your scent was on my gold," he stated with finality, as though the case were closed and all we awaited was sentencing.

The dragon gazed at us for a moment in silence, his eyes a rich yellow, the pupils wide black diamonds in the night that resembled a cat's or snake's eyes. The dragon's focus was severe and unwavering. He possessed that same egotistical, all-knowing smirk,

109

the smile ringing his eyes and mouth. We felt like our minds were being read.

He turned slowly to the burglar beside us, who, to his credit, remained rooted to the spot. "So was yours." The dragon's eyes narrowed, and any mirth that had been present on his face disappeared in a moment.

His voice exploded, rising in a quick crescendo, "Your scent is also in my lair!"

Without warning, the dragon reached out a claw the size of a large wheelbarrow and grabbed the burglar, slamming the man to the earth beside him in one definitive motion that left no doubt as to his fate. He had not even had time to cry out. Perhaps this was a small mercy.

My brother and I moved closer together and grabbed hold of each other's hands.

"We didn't touch your gold!" I called out with a loud voice. I refused to believe that a beast this intelligent could not be reasoned with. "They hid it in our ... our hermitage!"

The dragon had momentarily closed his eyes, savouring the revenge he had just exacted. He smiled his confident, self-satisfied smile, and leaned over to stare carefully into my eyes. A thousand years of mayhem I saw then, a cold, calculating conscious-ness that accepted the folly of man and the fates as much as the mystery surrounding life as simply so much pointless noise. His eyes revealed amusement at the futility of love, and mocked all who strove to reach higher toward the heavens, be it in searching for wisdom or in building anything with prayerful hope.

He sniffed me lightly, and reached out with a talon, the talon being the length of garden shears. He removed my toque with the same gentleness with which he had retrieved his gold from the snow days earlier, and ran the side of a talon along my hair and cheek with a touch as light as a butterfly's wing. I winced distastefully at this intimacy, knowing this foul claw was responsible for the death of my neighbours.

"You are young. Innocent. Young, innocent flesh is always the best," he whispered. "The taste of fallen man is always gamey for my palate." His breath was hot. I felt like I was standing in the glowing ring of a bonfire.

I looked at him with despair. I understood that I was on the verge of death, threatened by an utterly unreasonable being.

"Why?" shouted my brother, indignant at the illogic of it all. As far as he was concerned, justice had been served. My brother was innocence personified. I felt somewhere in the middle of this. My heart was torn. Glancing at my brother's upturned face, I knew I could not claim such innocence for myself. At the same time, I was guided by a hope that rejected any lust for power or pleasure.

The dragon looked to my brother and smiled again, but now I sensed that the smile was different. The cold, egotistical smile had been replaced by a wistful smile that suggested a change of heart.

He gazed from my brother back to me. In a clear whisper, he spoke to me alone. "I have learned many tongues of man. I have heard many tales. I have seen butchering in the time of Herod and Caesar, and I felt the earth shake while I slept, when bombs bright as the sun destroyed whole cities. I have watched the ceaseless march of man over the earth. I have seen kingdoms rise and I have seen them fall. I have flown high over ancient mountains peopled by lost, wandering tribes never to be remembered, and I have seen the moon glimmering on the ocean as sailors took their last gasp before slipping into the depths."

The dragon's wistful smile had faded away, replaced by a frustrated rage, his eyebrows angled fiercely, his large nostrils flaring. He reached out and scraped our icy cathedral roof with a tension that seemed ready to explode at any moment. But as he continued to draw lines across the gleaming ice with his black talons, he grew thoughtful.

"I have destroyed every man I ever met. And I have eaten many hermits in their hermitages. I regretted it, sometimes. On occasion, the hermits were ... rooted and innocent like you. They did not flee in terror. They did not carry the stench of corruption.

They were quiet. They could feel the earth. They understood the laws that govern man."

He looked at me carefully. "Do you, I wonder, know the rules that govern your life?" He didn't wait for me to answer. "Treasure, and the attaining of treasure, by whatever means." He looked at me triumphantly. "With the exception of an occasional, insignificant hero," he added derisively, "this rule governs the entire race of man. Scoundrels!"

"I have no desire for riches," I said stubbornly and self-righteously, pride welling in my heart. I had never craved gold or riches in my life.

The dragon shook his head impatiently, taking me for a dullard. "The treasure you seek takes many forms. Including haughty pride, young fool! And you will kill to achieve your desires." The dragon smiled his self-satisfied smile.

"I would never kill anyone, or anything!" I said, aware of the fact that his shifting language had given me pause to think.

"Like the earthly treasures that will possess your soul, killing also takes many forms." The dragon spoke slyly, but his eyes momentarily fell as though to hide a secret. In that instant, it dawned on me that the dragon had the capacity to be a noble creature. However corrupt his soul had become, there was a grain of goodness still dwelling within him. As if to brush off my searching of his soul, the dragon swung his head away in order to inspect the smuggler still in his grasp.

"Are you going to kill us?" my brother gasped. I noticed for the first time that we were both trembling violently.

The dragon turned to us once again and leaned in so that we could have reached out to touch his rigid nose with its large, slanting nostrils. My brother and I stood straight, petrified with fear, and prepared ourselves for a quick strike.

The dragon looked at my brother, and then moved his head slightly to look into my eyes. Now he neither moved nor blinked. His gaze penetrated my fear and even my awareness of self. I was lost in his being, floating in it like a dried leaf in a running stream. It was then that I came to an astounding realization, or better said, it was then that I began to understand what it was the dragon was trying to communicate to me.

"You are dying!" I exclaimed breathlessly.

The dragon's face did not change its stolid appearance, but his eyes flickered for the briefest moment like a candle's light in a faintly felt draught.

"There are other dragons, in many different forms," he began again, rising up and reasserting his will over us. "I have a new lair, where I will hope to enter into an endless slumber."

It was as though he were trying to reassure me, but still he looked at me, his expression changing now into one of longing.

"All I have seen ..." he began, and stopped himself. He snarled and grit his teeth together. His long fangs were fully revealed. Steam began to issue forth from his mouth and nostrils, forcing my brother and me to stumble backwards.

I had a vision of my brother running up and hugging the dragon. And I had a vision of offering a blessing upon his furrowed brow. The dragon's longing look revealed an immense frustration. He was questioning the heavens. He was asking the timeless questions we who are sensitive to our nature will ask without hope of response: Why? Why am I here? What happens when I die? How does eternity hold onto me?

The dragon chortled deep in his throat as he rose up to his full height, the flexing of his scale-encrusted body sounding like trees splintering or ice cracking. He had sensed my heart, and now disregarded my romantic wonderings.

"You would redeem me?" he asked mockingly. "All is waste!" he yelled, his resounding voice shaking the ground.

His voice, remaining strong and menacing, nevertheless quieted somewhat as he pierced me one final time with his intentional look. "All, but for this. You, hermit girl, will now remember and know."

The dragon thus betrayed himself in his moment of weakness. He was trapped in his own anger and frustration, but even as he prepared to die in hibernation, he could not help expressing hope. It was a hope that he would be remembered, a hope that something would grow from his return to dust and ash. I stared into the dragon's eyes with a somber affirmation and bowed ever so slightly, as though in ritual he had passed over to me a sacred vessel.

With a look of shocking disbelief over betraying himself, of revealing his soul and its inherent doubt to a girl, he recoiled in fright. Throwing us to the ground with the force of his sweeping, shuddering wings, the dragon bounded into the Christmas night. In an instant, he was a vague shadow lost in the light of a smattering of distant stars. I never learned his name.

My brother and I stole a glance at where the dragon's claw had pinned the thief, but there was no sign of him. We no longer had any desire to re-enter the snow cathedral, and never did return to its shelter. One sunny day during Christmas break friends led us to our yard, and though they delighted in the snow cavern and tunnels, my brother and I meandered about at the foundation of our former home until they grew frustrated by our refusal to play along. We were not aware of it at the time, but in retrospect, we were suffering from the loss of a world, our old world, before the dragon.

We did not mourn for this ancient beast, but we understood with an instinctive clarity that our lives were governed by universal laws. Since being confronted by the dragon's judgment of the human race, we have fervently desired to better the dragon by not being scoundrels. The dragon had turned from the light. Not us. Reach for the light, and in so doing you will be guided by it. The hero accepts this responsibility in time. It is a labour of love.